MW01474336

THE BUTCHER, THE BAKER, AND THE EVIL SPY MAKER

JEANNE ESCE

LifeRich
PUBLISHING®

Copyright © 2020 Jeanne Esce.

All rights reserved. No part of this book may be used or reproduced by any means, graphic, electronic, or mechanical, including photocopying, recording, taping or by any information storage retrieval system without the written permission of the author except in the case of brief quotations embodied in critical articles and reviews.

This is a work of fiction. All of the characters, names, incidents, organizations, and dialogue in this novel are either the products of the author's imagination or are used fictitiously.

LifeRich Publishing is a registered trademark of The Reader's Digest Association, Inc.

LifeRich Publishing books may be ordered through booksellers or by contacting:

LifeRich Publishing
1663 Liberty Drive
Bloomington, IN 47403
www.liferichpublishing.com
1 (888) 238-8637

Because of the dynamic nature of the Internet, any web addresses or links contained in this book may have changed since publication and may no longer be valid. The views expressed in this work are solely those of the author and do not necessarily reflect the views of the publisher, and the publisher hereby disclaims any responsibility for them.

Any people depicted in stock imagery provided by Getty Images are models, and such images are being used for illustrative purposes only. Certain stock imagery © Getty Images.

ISBN: 978-1-4897-3015-2 (sc)
ISBN: 978-1-4897-3025-1 (e)

Library of Congress Control Number: 2020915095

Print information available on the last page.

LifeRich Publishing rev. date: 08/10/2020

CHAPTER 1

ELLEN HEARD THE music rising out of her foggy sleep and rolled over to see with one eye, that her husband was dutifully rising and stumbling into the bathroom. After he had punched the alarm off, she could have written a symphony of dull music from his steady rhythmic steps entering the start of his new day. Like clockwork, her husband, Daniel, was always the same. There were the same number of steps into the bathroom, the same rhythm to his gait... same, same, same. She did not know how one human being could go through his life so robotically and not go stark raving mad.

As she lazed in bed, undecided as to whether to rouse herself or not, she stared at the ceiling and listened to his ritualistic movements even with the bathroom door closed. Like a metronome she directed her mind to the sound of the water as he brushed his teeth, and then prepared to shave before his shower. He was truly a man stuck in the routine rhythm of everyday life. She could count on his sameness. He never varied his routine which in itself brought a certain assurance but she loathed the blasé and lackluster time. It reminded her of the song "Is that all there is?"

As she laid there reminiscing about the old days, when she was younger, more attractive and much more vital, she couldn't help but feel left out of things. In the old days there was travel, great clothes, excitement, fine food, good wine and being noticed as striking. And now here she lay, weary, depressed, unmotivated, overweight, and fed up with her existence. There was a lot to say about the effects of menopause and the psychological outlook on life. The physiological changes were bad enough but the fact that being empty nested went hand in hand with all of the trauma, - was a lot for most women to take. When Ellen was in her prime, she had a career, plans for the future and an interesting life. She had excitement and adventure. Then she met Daniel.

Little did she know that by meeting Daniel, her life would change so drastically. She thought she had her life mapped out and her future certain. Ellen had been disappointed in men and had had some tragic endings. She lost her trust and because of the pain, she decided that she would rather stay single and travel the world. She would live where she wanted and live how she wanted. She had a good paying job and she could make her own plans.

But Daniel had other ideas.

CHAPTER 2

DANIEL MICHAEL DINATO was an Italian American from Buffalo, NY. The eldest of four children of Italian immigrants, Daniel was the first of his family to go to college. There was a large celebration when Daniel was accepted into Notre Dame. The whole family was ecstatic. And "family" is the way to describe it. Daniel's father was the eldest of eight and his mother was the youngest of five. Family gatherings which were always a weekly event, were full of food, fun, and laughter. Someone was always celebrating a birthday or event and their world was the family. Their whole social life was because of family and there was no more room for anything else. Just like it is depicted in the movies, there were never quiet times when they got together. When a meal was served there was always room for one more and meals lasted for hours. The problems of the world or at least the neighborhood were solved at these dinner tables.

Children knew they were adored, and they were so special in their family's eyes. However, the families were also strict disciplinarians. It was not unusual to get hit up the side of the head if someone transgressed. And church was extremely important. If the boys were old enough, they usually served as altar boys. And there were no excuses to miss mass unless someone was on their deathbed. The smell of sauce (*or gravy as some of the families called it) would welcome them home from church and then the extended family would start descending. Dining tables had to be huge and the chairs didn't all match, but no one cared. Everyone pitched in to help, but the hostess always made the sauce, pasta and meat.

Holidays were prepared for, days in advance. Easter pies, pastries and treats were made in multitudes. On Christmas Eve, the Feast of the Seven Fishes was something planned for weeks ahead of time. Traditions were passed down from generation to generation and respected by all ages. And no one ever left hungry.

Daniel enjoyed a typical Italian family upbringing and knew from an early age that he was expected to go to college. He was the shining example of the American dream. Going away to school was a point of pride and accomplishment for the whole family. When Daniel graduated from Notre Dame he had to fulfill his ROTC commitment. During his four years of college he worked at his Army plan to serve when he was done. However, the Vietnam conflict was raging at the time, and his family was very fearful that he would be shipped off to Asia. Their prayers were answered when he was assigned to Germany after his basic training. Everyone was so relieved because Germany would put him out of harms way.

It also would allow him to travel to Italy to visit relatives who still lived in the "homeland". As often happens, Daniel's family had been so busy living the American dream that they did not have the time to travel back to those relatives they remembered so kindly. Letters, pictures and cards had to suffice.

Unlike the typical Italian American depicted in the movies, Daniel was unusual. He was quiet, devout and serious. He took his faith very seriously and had even pondered becoming a priest. After much consideration, he realized that he enjoyed female companionship more and had always wanted to have his own family. He took his family and his commitments quite seriously but could still go out and have a beer with the guys. He was a deep thinker and very analytical. But with a past with his Italian family, he knew how to have a good time.

Ellen on the other hand was just the opposite. She was definitely more gregarious and outgoing. Ellen was raised in the Midwest with a small conservative family. It was almost as if the two had been switched in the hospital nursery and given to the opposite families.

Ellen had a joie de vivre that couldn't be suppressed. In fact, her energy level and high jinks left her parents stumped. The family physician even put Ellen on tranquilizers at the age of 15 at the request of her parents because the family was being driven crazy by her constant movement and activity. They didn't realize that she was a spirited typical teenager with lots of energy. Her family just never got Ellen and she had always looked forward to a time when she could fit in with a spirited family who would not be repelled by her behaviors.

Ellen's sister conformed to the quieter, more conservative setting of Ellen's family. She preferred watching TV and quietly reading to going outside and playing King of the Mountain or tag. The older Ellen got, the gap in their relationship got even wider. They were two totally different people. She had an older brother who learned at an early age to find something to occupy his waking hours. He was rarely home and when he was, he kept to himself. Living in the Midwest, she began to realize that there were discrepancies in what they were taught in church and <u>what</u> they lived in the small town.

Her first lesson in discrimination came when she was about 14. The 9,000 people who inhabited their town were pretty WASPish. There were three token Jewish families, many Christians of American descent, several Catholic families, some German Lutherans, four Italian families, no Asians, and absolutely no African Americans. When Ellen had been down attending her Junior Lifesaving certificate, she noticed one of her teachers who was responsible for the waterfront and concession stand at the town lake, approach two car loads of African American ladies and their children from a near-by larger town. He immediately notified the ladies that they were not allowed at our private lake. This lake was for town's people only. He then told them that they could go out to the edge of town and swim at that lake which I knew was our town's sewage disposal lake. Ellen was horrified and when she got home she asked her parents about this incident. They told her that they never had discussed this with the children because they personally found it distasteful, but that there was an unwritten law, an understanding of all of the town's people, that the sun did not set if there was a black person there. This did not make sense to Ellen and she never forgot her first lesson in how cruel and discriminatory people could be.

Ironically this same discrimination carried over to Daniel when Ellen married him. In some members of her community, Daniel was less than American and was from one of those countries over there. Several snide comments were made when Ellen's engagement notice was in the paper. They couldn't believe that Ellen's family was happy about the coming wedding.

Another lesson Ellen learned which she noticed through her entire life was about the subject of the "Haves" and the "Have Nots". Certainly in a rural community in the Midwest there were the "Haves" and the "Have Nots". In fact there was a third category which she learned all too early in life and they were the "Have Lots". In life there is a natural pecking order which is established in society. There are people who are in need and who live by struggling for their existence. They don't necessarily have to be dirt poor, but seem to always have to be fraught with financial worries and stresses. Next there are people who have the ability to pay their bills and are comfortable in their daily existence. And lastly there are those people who seem to always have more than the vast majority. They are the ones who have designer clothes, fancy cars and vacations, and larger homes. At first Ellen thought that it was because it was small town living which caused such a delineation. She reflected that the differences were marked and obvious with a smaller population, but even when she lived in larger places, the demarcation was still apparent. From an early age, she realized that she was considered to be just a "Have". The "Have Lots" children and adults of her small town wasted no time in making it apparent that they had more. The "Have Lots" used their superior attitude as a weapon to bully. This did not change with age or location.

There is something to be said about living in a small town where everyone knows your business. The advantage is that there were neighbors who were there in a crisis to help and commiserate. However there is also something to be said about the indifference of the city and anonymity.

In a small town it was obvious who dressed well and who did not. Being a "Have" was not as traumatic as being a "Have Not". There were actually children in Ellen's school who lived in tar paper shacks with dirt floors. There was a timid little girl in the third grade with Ellen who lived in just such a home. She asked Ellen if she would like to play with her after school and Ellen agreed. As they were walking the three blocks home to Ellen's house, they passed the mom and pop neighborhood grocery store. The little girl told Ellen that her mother had given her a nickel to spend at the store for a candy treat. Ellen was so shocked because she knew the little girl was so poor that the nickel was a big sacrifice for this girl's family. She was so touched by this example of giving unselfishly, she never forgot it. This was one of the children that would get heckled for wearing old hand-me-downs and patched clothing and from that time on Ellen would stand up to the bullies and support the down trodden.

In her small town, the discrimination didn't stop at homes or clothing; the bullies would pick on the vulnerable, unmercifully. One evening after supper, Ellen was invited down to a neighbor's house to "play". In the" Have Lots" girl's bedroom, the bully asked Ellen what she thought of certain classmates. Ellen wanted to be kind and not controversial, so she told the bully that she liked them all. The bully kept prodding Ellen to say something, anything against one of her friends. So Ellen thought for a while and finally decided to say something negative. The most she could come up with was that this certain girl thought she was smarter than the rest of her classmates. At that very moment, that certain classmate crawled out from underneath the bully's bed and laughed in Ellen's face. The lesson Ellen learned the hard way was to not be bullied into saying something you do not want to say. And to always live by the old adage of, "If you cannot say something nice, do not say anything at all".

Ellen was subjected to the classless cliques of the nouveau riche in her little town. On numerous occasions Ellen would disappear into her bedroom to shed the tears of frustration and humiliation. Unfortunately, when the small group of little minds decided to strike with their pretentious personalities they would plow right over anyone in their path. Their attire may have been more costly, but their lack of good manners and thoughtfulness were more than evident. Even though Ellen did not realize this at the time, she would later learn that this pecking order had been happening for centuries and the people that have been hurt and will continue to be hurt are too numerous to count. It is very sad that the "Have Lots", in their attempts to show how much better they are than everyone else, only show everyone how lacking they are in true class. When their glitter is gone, all that is left are their true colors of their conceited ways. She would learn as time went on, that these people were to be pitied because their lives were lived in the vain attempt to pretend and to act superior at all times. She would soon learn when she went to college and after, that it had to be exhausting for them to always play that part.

As an end result of the sum of her early life experiences, Ellen had a tough time trusting people until they proved themselves to be trust worthy. This was counter to her attitude of always trying to be happy. She definitely had mixed emotions about the "Have Lots", and decided very early on that she was just fine being a "Have", and she also was determined to try to always be kind and helpful to the "Have Nots"

This decision was probably why Ellen finally decided to go into Education. With her empathy for people, she was a natural for teaching and nurturing. Her boundless energy didn't hurt either. She needed that strength to take care of a classroom of young children and guide them along their way. Her early life lessons would prove to be very important in forming who she became and why. She was a very determined young lady.

CHAPTER 3

INITIALLY WHEN ELLEN decided to go to college she wanted to get a job in Paris and work for the government overseas. This came out of an early experience with a teenaged babysitter who was studying French in high school. She practiced on Ellen and Ellen was automatically enamored. Even at five, Ellen thought that French was romantic and mysterious. She was also interested in psychology so she decided on a double major. She attended Indiana University and majored in both.

However it wasn't long before the United States was ordered out of France along with all of its bases and there went her future job. Or so she thought. So being a young woman who needed a job with some security, she chose to switch to education and she lost nothing in the transition. Ellen was lucky enough to go on to get a Masters in Special Education in Learning Disabilities when it was in its infancy. After graduation she was very fortunate because very few people had this degree. At this point in time she could write her own ticket to anywhere. She started to have nightmares about her fortunate predicament however, and continued to have these same nightmares years later. The thought of having no direction was troubling. Never the less, Ellen remembered an undergrad professor whom she really admired and whom had discussed her past teaching experience with at the Department of Defense. She learned that every accompanied tour of duty requires the government to teach the dependent children of service people. Ellen boldly contacted the DOD and requested an application. She was pleasantly surprised when she was automatically accepted. Usually, the DOD required incoming new teachers to serve a two year hardship assignment in a faraway place in some not so nice locales. But as luck would have it, they placed her in Germany. She said goodbye to all her friends and family and embarked on a brand new journey in a strange new home. She found herself in a brand new country, with a brand new language and lifestyle. She was nervous but very excited to experience all that this new world had to offer. Little did she know that her life would take a dramatic shift in direction. And, a new person would walk into her life and change the plans she had so carefully laid out.

Daniel Dinato graduated with an Electrical Engineering degree from Notre Dame and an MBA from Purdue. When he was ready to serve his military obligation from ROTC he looked forward to being stationed overseas. As luck would have it, he was one of the lucky few who were sent to Germany. With his Italian background he anticipated travelling and visiting with his relatives. With great anticipation, he arrived in Germany in January. After settling into to his BOQ apartment (Bachelor Officer Quarters), he returned from the commissary and PX with much needed supplies. As he walked down the hall he spied an attractive young lady going into her apartment right across from his place.

(The single teachers were billeted in the BOQ also, which made for easy dating opportunities.) Ironically Ellen had absolutely no intention of getting entangled in a relationship and had her plans for the next few years all set. Her plans included travel, travel, and more travel. However on his first fateful day at his new home, their lives would take on a new path.

Just as he was walking down the hall he unknowingly spotted his future. The first thing he noticed were her legs. He admired her carefree stance and ease of movement. She looked like a dancer. And then she disappeared inside her apartment without noticing him. Not being very experienced in meeting girls, Daniel racked his brain as to how he could introduce himself. He had dated in college and had had a couple of girlfriends, but he was far more serious about his studies. He arrived in Germany with no strings attached. But for some reason, this girl intrigued him. Daniel got up his courage and knocked on her door. When she answered, Daniel stood there with a bottle of Scotch in one hand and a crystal glass in the other and shyly introduced himself and requested some ice. And that is how he met Ellen. As Ellen opened her door, she displayed that honest, open Midwestern, never met a stranger openness and broke into a broad smile.

Ellen introduced herself and welcomed him to his new home country. She invited him in and automatically filled his glass with ice and he sipped his Scotch. She offered him a seat and made herself her own favorite drink, a martini. Even though they were from such different backgrounds, different religions, different ethnic cultures, they found their conversation easy. As the days went by, Daniel found himself knocking on Ellen's door every afternoon. After work, it was standard behavior for all of the singles in the BOQ to leave their doors open to appear hospitable. If she wasn't home, he would step into the hallway and listen for her laugh. He would then follow her laugh until he found her.

It was not Ellen's intention to settle down with anyone. She was there to do her job, enjoy her new country and travel as much as she could. She had her future planned out. She would spend the next two years teaching in Germany and them return to the U.S. and finish her PhD. She did not want to be tied down with anyone or anything. She wanted her freedom. However, even though Ellen was casually dating other officers, she kept coming back to Daniel's invitations. After a great deal of time and soul searching, she decided that Daniel, even with all of his differences, made more sense than any man she had ever dated. Even though he was Catholic, Italian, and from a completely different culture, she felt that he was the one who she should be with – forever. Within the year he overcame his shyness and popped the question. He knew how serious she was about her future plans but when asking her to marry him, he asked what it would take to change her mind. Ellen just smiled and told him she already had.

They were married six months later back in the States and immediately flew back to Germany to finish both of their commitments. They then called their stay in Germany and later in Italy, their honeymoon on the U. S. government. After their assignments were up, they decided to move to Italy and immerse themselves in that culture before returning to the States and work.

Their time in Europe was blissful, carefree, and exciting. Since Daniel did not have to be back to the United States quickly, they took this opportunity to live in Italy where some of his relatives still lived. It just so happened that they lived on the Italian Riviera and they lived the dolce vita – the sweet life. This was another opportunity for Daniel to practice his Italian and for Ellen to learn a new language. His relatives were very welcoming and seemed to enjoy teaching Ellen about their culture and their language. They spent their days lounging at the beach and drinking wine and their nights trying to start their family. It was heavenly and they both forgot that the real world was waiting for them to return and start their real life of work, responsibilities, and life.

CHAPTER 4

WHAT ELLEN DIDN'T realize when she married Daniel was that he had one persona for the Army, Europe, and being newly married and another totally different mindset for his future career. The long second honeymoon living in Italy was enough to distort her view of Daniel's personality. With nothing but leisure time they loved being footloose and carefree. But they also knew that that time would come screeching to a halt when reality set in and they returned to his job in the United States. Often they would remark that they could never duplicate this happy-go-lucky time in their future and that they should cherish the time that they had. They did not take it for granted.

Soon the couple was moving back to the states and starting a new exciting life together, but what had been relaxed and carefree, now took on a life of its own. Ellen learned very quickly that Daniel was very serious about his job and his future. Even though they were trying to start a family, Daniel's main focus was work. She soon found out the true meaning of a workaholic and had to try to fit into Daniel's life.

Before long Ellen was setting up a nursery and overjoyed at the idea of motherhood. Their first son was born with unusual red hair, and he soon learned to tell people he got the red hair from the milkman even though he did not know what that really meant. Ellen soon learned that there are redheaded Italians. The next son was born with darker skin, dark eyes and more Italian features. And the last son was born a toe-head with blue eyes,

And she explained to any who would remark, that they had genetic potpourri. She would have loved to have found out what the next one could have been, but God had other plans. Their first son was named Santino (Sonny for short). Their second was named Dante (Danny) and the third was Franco (Frankie). Because Daniel's job was full of opportunity for advancement, Daniel made a steady climb in the company. They never lived long enough in one place to even renew their drivers' licenses.

The Dinato household was as lively as Ellen and Daniel could imagine. They were always the magnet house with the back door slamming dozens of times a day. Wherever they moved, the Dinato household became "the" place to be. Their grocery bill was horrendous but they were happy that their sons wanted to be at their own house with their friends to play, so it worked out just fine.

Daniel was a successful business executive and he worked very hard to provide for his family, but his job kept him on the road all week long. Even when he was in town at his office he was always thinking business. To Ellen his job was like his mistress. He knew he had a family but that pull of something else was ever present. So Ellen became the mom that could be counted on to be room mother, taxi, PTA committee member, and whatever else people needed. Ellen threw herself into being a mom as her number one job. She had learned through her studies that being a stay at home mom was the most underrated (but crucial) job with no compensation except knowing that she was raising good solid boys. Even though she usually saw the boys on the fly, she was there to tuck them in at night and listen to their thoughts.

Family dinner with or without dad was another very important and necessary connection of raising the boys. Ellen found out by listening to their conversations about what was happening in their school and to them and their friends. She never resented the fact that other women were dressing up to go to work while she was in the scruffs most of the time. She knew deep down that what she was doing was important and vital. Parents seldom get a report card for their parenting, but she enjoyed the frequent comments about the boys' manners and respect. Parents have a long wait to see if their work has paid off. The glimpses of success and pride do happen, but not nearly often enough.

CHAPTER 5

THE YEARS FLEW by with school, church, sports, and Boy Scouts. All three boys were able to achieve Eagle Scout, get their first communion, confirmation, and study to prepare for college. Her sons were not the students that Daniel and Ellen were but they also weren't raised with as much stress to excel. The main thing they wanted for their boys was for them to be healthy, happy and well rounded. And they were.

With the boys college bound, Ellen started to think about the future. No longer able to have children, Ellen even thought about adopting, but Daniel wasn't keen on the subject. She could get a job or do crafts or a dozen other activities, but her heart wasn't in it.

One afternoon, tired from running errands and starting dinner, Ellen decided to take a nap. She had roughly an hour to close her eyes and rest before her youngest came home from school. As she slept she had a dream. The dream was vivid and long. It was like watching a movie. It was in color and the story was compelling. When she awoke she remembered the dream and was amazed at its clarity. She had been playing around with the idea of writing a book for a long while, because she loved writing, but she discouraged herself from the idea because she did not know the first thing about getting a book published. She had ideas, but did not know where to go from there. Ellen researched and asked others until she felt confident that she knew what she was doing. Again she started into a new adventure in a new land. She had the plot and even the title, all from vivid dreams.

CHAPTER 6

WRITING A BOOK turned into Ellen's cause celebre. She would write and rewrite when the house was quiet. She actually liked the solitude and the thoughts and ideas poured out of her fingers as she typed on her computer. She had typed enough college assignments, final reports for the boys and business letters for her husband that she felt quite proficient at typing. The computer had become Ellen's new best friend.

To begin, Ellen put all her memories from her dream down on paper and then she made a time line on a poster which helped her follow the order of events. Knowing that she was a total novice at this endeavor made it all the more inviting because she didn't know if she was doing things correctly or not. Having read hundreds of books in her life didn't totally prepare her for writing one. So she just dove in. She knew she didn't have anything to lose except that pesky boredom that seemed to want to consume her.

The dream which she was using as the basis for her plot dealt with a mundane housewife who was nearly empty nested and bored to tears, tired of volunteering and lost with no identity. This desperate housewife was married to a kind, considerate, workaholic who gave his life's blood to his work. The idea of retirement looming off in the distance made both of them frightened because the housewife, whom she named Emily and the workaholic whom she named Douglas DiLallo, questioned about what in the world they were going to do in a house with each other, alone 24 hours a day for the rest of their lives. Emily thought that Douglas would just be found slumped on top of spread sheets at his desk someday with his cell phone in one hand and his Chrome book in the other, dead as a door nail. Writing the descriptions of her lead characters was so easy because it was semi-auto-biographable. There was no stretch of the imagination. She had lived in this body and with this workaholic almost her entire married life.

Ellen even used her own setting of Upstate New York for the book's location. The home that Ellen and Daniel had designed and built ironically turned into the home that they inhabited for more years than any other in both of their lives. When they built their house in New York, they had decided that the moving would stop and the roots would go down. And so it was easy and comfortable to use this home as Emily and Douglas's.

Douglas was the same plodding, business driven person as Daniel. Emily was identical to Ellen in thought, word and deed. She merely had to plug in new names to describe their daily comings and goings.

The plot dealt with the fact that Douglas had a typical corporate job, but a second, covert life. The many espionage and spy books that Ellen had read allowed her to know that the best covert person was a non-descript, easy going, and blasé person. That was how she wrote Douglas. He had the same traits as Daniel but that is where the similarities ended. She wrote that Douglas also went to college at a prestigious school and went on to get his MBA, but he was recruited not by the FBI as were some of his law school buddies, but by a no-named agency that didn't make much sense at the time but seemed glamorous and exciting to a 24 year old. A distinguished gentleman had called on him at school and set up an appointment to talk about his future. He explained that Douglas had been vetted and that he came out squeaky clean. And this gentleman had a proposition for him. Douglas was also intrigued and complimented to be chosen and felt good about the possibility of helping out his country in any way he could. All he knew was that he would be contacted at a later date by a Mr. Larabee and he was to do exactly what Mr. Larabee told him to do. For this he would be remunerated secretly in an account in a bank in the British West Indies. It took a year for Douglas to hear from "Mr. Larabee", whom he almost forgot was going to contact him. When Douglas answered the phone on a busy Monday at work, a gentleman told him that he was returning his call (in case the conversation was being recorded) and that this was Mr. Larabee. Douglas racked his brain to try to remember who he had called by that name within the last few days and couldn't for the life of him remember anyone by that name and then after a few seconds of pause it dawned on him exactly who this was. "Good afternoon Mr. Larabee, thank you for returning my call." Mr. Larabee proceeded to explain that he was having some paper work over-nighted to his home and that Douglas could peruse the information about their next meeting. Mr. Larabee further explained that the papers were mistakenly sent to his home because he accidentally used his home address instead of his office and he apologized for that snafu. Douglas thanked him not knowing what in the world this was all about but was captivated beyond belief.

When Douglas arrived home that evening from work there was a large envelope marked personal along with all of the rest of the mail waiting for him on the hall table. The "personal" document that arrived for Douglas he immediately took up to the master bedroom, changed out of his work clothes and forever changed his life.

After changing into his relaxing clothes, Douglas opened the envelope from Mr. Larabee and pored over the business letter that was no different than many others he received in his business life but he knew it had a different meaning. The letter was a nondescript letter, if read by anyone else would seem to be about contract negotiations, but in the end there was a paragraph that explained that in the future all negotiations would be handled by a Mr. Essex and that all future communications would be handled through this gentleman. Mr. Larabee explained that he was retiring and that Mr. Essex had been promoted to take his place. It was all very business- like and all very ordinary. If intercepted and read by anyone else it was just a business letter, but to Douglas, it was the beginning of a double life.

Two days later a Mr. Essex called at his home and introduced himself as Mr. Larabee's replacement in his company. Douglas knew instantly who it was and played along as he should, and listened intently. Mr. Essex explained that he knew from his itinerary that Douglas traveled monthly to San Francisco to corporate offices. Douglas was amazed that someone else besides himself, his family and the company's travel agent knew what his schedule was. But he knew he was dealing with people who could find out all kinds of things that the ordinary person could not. Mr. Essex further explained that he knew that Douglas stayed at the extended stay apartment that his company always rented for him on his trips to California. The apartment was so much nicer than staying in a hotel and it even allowed him to leave his laundry there and have fresh clean clothes waiting for him upon his return. He even left personal objects and family photos because he was the only one using the apartment.

Mr. Essex further explained that there would be a fresh basket of fruit left for him upon his arrival to his apartment. Douglas couldn't figure out what fruit had to do with anything but he went along with the explanation. Sure enough, upon his arrival in San Francisco and his apartment he found a lovely basket of fruit. Attached to the basket was a card and inside the card it explained to him that if he wanted to thank the basket-giver, that he should call 1-800-555-2390. Douglas's curiosity was peaked and he immediately called the number. The gentleman who answered asked who Douglas wished to speak to. After a few awkward seconds, Douglas stumbled and replied, "I think I need to speak to Mr. Essex. "Ah," said the voice at the other end, "This is Mr. Essex and I have been waiting for your call. I understand you just received your fruit. Then we will make sure that you receive fruit upon each visit. And actually if you notice bananas included in your fruit basket we want you to take the plastic liner in the bottom of the basket with you back to New York and leave it in the bathroom of the first rest stop on the thruway on your way home from the airport. You will find a permanent wall fixture that is for trash in the men's room. Please place the plastic liner in between the clear plastic bag of the container and the metal wall of the fixture."

Douglas listened in awe because he was actually participating in something so mysterious. And sure enough there were bananas included in his fruit basket. He waited hesitantly all week long and couldn't wait to see what would happen. Upon his return to New York, he collected his car from his car service and got on the road. At the very first road stop he got off the highway and went into the men's room where he indeed found the waste receptacle. He looked around to see if anyone was there and carefully pulled out the plastic liner (the size of 81/2 by 11 paper) from his sport coat and placed it in between the wall of the container and the plastic garbage bag. And he was done. Job finished, now what? He washed his hands ritualistically as if getting rid of his dirty business and went on his merry way.

His next trip to California found the fruit basket in place and a card attached. It again explained that he should call the 800 number to the gift giver. When he did, Mr. Essex congratulated him on a job well done. He said that when he received a birthday card from his insurance company next month, that there would be a series of numbers on the back of the card that did not represent the price of the card but his own personal off-shore account that would receive a $500 dollar deposit for each transaction. In the beginning Douglas was excited by his additional money which he and Emily could use upon retirement. He could always explain that he had been given a trust fund by an aunt or something and that he had been letting the money collect interest and now they had a nice nest egg and money enough for them to buy that beach house they had always wanted. In the years that followed, the money got even better and he was amassing quite a large nest egg.

The modus operandi got more complicated and he was delivering different things. Mr. Essex even got his hands on someone within the New York state thruway system and was able to place a smiley face on the EZPass right lane sign above the toll booth that Douglas used to and from the airport. If the smiley face was there it meant that he would not deliver whatever was in the bottom of the fruit basket and would wait until next time and then deliver two liners. That only happened twice. After several years passed Mr. Essex, who Douglas could never describe if asked, sent him some Notre Dame sticker pennants for his luggage. Douglas always had a fancy luggage tag with his personal information on it attached to his suitcase. But with the pennants on, his suitcase was easily identifiable. Since he always took the same flights to California and back, it was easy for someone to place something next to his pennant on his suitcase. If there was that same smiley face adhered to the luggage he knew to call the 800 number. He would rip it off when he arrived and wait until another one was placed on his luggage.

As the years passed his tasks would vary from time to time but they were never anything he considered dangerous or even scary – just intriguing. He proceeded along in his business life doing his job very well and getting promotions. A few times the promotions dealt with moves to other locations but by the time they came, his three sons were ensconced in their schools with their friends and didn't want to leave. Douglas had heard too many stories of children rebelling and going wrong because of such upheaval and stories of numerous divorces because the wives couldn't take moving any more. So he and Emily wisely decided to stay put. Only once did they have to say no to a move because all of the other times the company redistricted so that Douglas could keep his region and his home base in New York.

(When Ellen was writing this section she wished that this was what had happened to her and Daniel. She was covetous of a staid life-style and a steady home front. So she added this part on purpose and it made the plot flow better. And the three sons were also easy although she also fantasized about making them girls and then decided against it. She really didn't know what it was like to raise girls.)

The basic plot of the book dealt with this ordinary man going about his ordinary life but having this secret part of something much bigger than he was. Years went by and Douglas did his duty to his job and his second life. The subplot was basically about a housewife who tried everything that she could think of to keep herself occupied and to not blow her brains out from sheer desperation and boredom. In a sense it had as much to do with suggestions she had tried to keep from going bonkers and extremely anxious. So it was part espionage and part self-help for the baby boomers who were arriving at the same destination that she had.

Ellen enjoyed adding touches of sarcasm and humor to her writing which everyone has to have to get through life. She ended the book which was part James Bond and part Erma Bombeck with a surprise ending.

Twenty seven years after Douglas had started on his venture with this secret endeavor, his own uncle Sal died. The whole DiLallo family was gathered in the front parlor of their family home and the family lawyer, Uncle Nicky, read the will. Uncle Sal who died childless and a widower had worked very hard all his life at his butcher shop. Everyone loved him and he was the best butcher in town. He made his own sausage and even packaged his own sauce for people who were too busy to make it from scratch – which he thought was a sin. But he laughed all the way to the bank.

As Emily and Douglas sat there listening to Uncle Sal's and Aunt Carmella's life being divided up with the heirs, they sat in reverie of all the good times they had had at family events. Birthdays, Christenings, First communions, confirmations, weddings, or any excuse for a party, their memories flooded by. Suddenly Douglas was shaken from his daydreaming when he heard his name being pronounced. Uncle Nicky started to smile. He repeated Douglas's name, "To my favorite nephew who helped out unselfishly at our store and never wanted to take any money for his work, who would visit religiously when he came home from school and who shared his family with us as if we were the grandparents, I leave a bank account in the British West Indies. Yes, all these years you have given an old couple hours of fun devising new ways for you to have a little spice in your life. Spice that you needed, my serious one. Life is not all work and no play. Both Aunt Carmella, God rest her soul, and I wanted you to have some added zest and not take life so seriously. You are a good boy and we wanted you to have a little nest egg for your retirement. And believe me, now you can retire when you want to not when you have to. Take time to smell the roses and look around at those who love you. Your work can go in a fleeting minute and what are you left with? Just pay stubs and some memories. But your family is there for you everyday – all the days of your life. Enjoy!!!!"

It turned out that Uncle Sal had friends in many walks of life, people who worked baggage at the airport, for the thruway authority and many other places. It was a game for Carmella and Sal to come up with innovative ways to add some distraction for Douglas and some fun to his life. When the will was finished Douglas just sat there and laughed hysterically and the whole DiLallo family thought he must have lost his mind in grief. And later at dinner, he explained the whole story to the family who still discuss it at every family event. What a legacy from Uncle Sal.

Ellen loved the way the book ended. She thought the Italian humor was a cross between the movies <u>Moonstruck</u> and <u>My Great Big Fat Greek Wedding</u>. Italian or Greek - the humor was the same; the family closeness was the same. And she thought she had sent a message – that the book was actually substantive in addition to being entertaining.

As she had been writing she struggled with a title for

the book. She wanted the Douglas role to have a clever name and one that would represent covert activities. One afternoon, as she laid down for a nap, she was mulling this over in her head. As she slept, whether she heard the cawing of crows through her window or it came from deep within her subconscious, she awoke with the name, <u>The Crow</u>. Not only would Douglas have that as his code name, but that would be the title for her book. But as she was finalizing her editing, she heard on television a trailer for a new movie taken from a comic book character named <u>The Crow</u>. Brandon Lee was to play the part of "The Crow" and Ellen was devastated. "How could they do that', she fumed? 'That was my idea"! So she put it out of her mind for a day and periodically thought about her predicament. She decided that she could add an adjective and not step on any one's toes. So her new title was, <u>The Illusive Crow</u>. She was set to start her new foray into the book world.

Getting the book published was another thing entirely. People can write all day but to get it actually on the book stands would become a new education for Ellen. It actually took months. First she needed to find an agent. When she sifted through the large list of agents, she decided on two and she contacted them both. She finally chose the first one and she placed her future in his hands. He was located in New York City and she knew she could hop down for the day whenever she needed. The agent was finally able to find a publisher and for a first time author, she was bowled over to find that the publisher not only loved it, but was very excited about publishing it.

Ellen was absolutely amazed at the success of her

book. Usually, at a first printing, the book company will only produce a small number. Then they see how it fares. And then if it is popular, they will definitely do a second and further printing. It was quickly obvious that there would be an immediate second printing.

Because she loved writing the first book so much and she met with a victory, her editor urged her to write a new book. She was already one step ahead of them. She was already starting a new one. The book company enjoyed her humor and frankness; and the fact that she used everyday experiences to relate to her reading audience was a big plus. So once again she contemplated a new plot.

She didn't have to go far for a new theme. In real life, Ellen had always been intrigued by the family of her sister-in-law. They were dark and mysterious creatures and they scared her to death. When Ellen and Daniel had moved back to the United States, they met them for the first time. Ellen had just finished living in Germany for a couple of years and when she started speaking German to the couple, they very rudely shut her off and demanded that they spoke Dutch or English so speak to them only in English. That was truly odd because she had heard their only child, her sister-in-law, speak German to them and Ellen recognized the difference. To make matters worse, Ellen very naively mentioned that she was just finished reading the book, <u>The Rise and Fall of the Third Reich</u>, and she was literally screamed at that she was not to mention anything like that in their presence. Ellen was quite taken aback and realized one of two things must exist. One possibility was that the parents may have lived through a terrible chapter of history themselves or, two, they were actually involved in something too horrible to consider and they did not want to be exposed. This was not to be the only unfortunate scene that Ellen and Daniel were privy to. Throughout the next few years, they witnessed the unbalanced and bizarre behavior of the couple. The father, Willem Van Eyck got his jollies out of shaking people's hand until it was unbelievably painful and then he would sneer at them as he said hello. That alone was reason enough not to be around them, but the mother, Greta, did very unusual things to go out of her way to freak people out. One time, she was pouring wine and then she snickered and told how in her country if people didn't like you they would put poison or other vile things in your wine. And then she just laughed in a shrill, insane laugh that gave everyone the creeps. It did not take long for Daniel and Ellen to refuse to go to family gatherings where the "sick" ones were going to be. This avoidance didn't sit well with the other family members but they could hardly blame them because they were freaked out as well, but caught in a very uncomfortable position.

Ellen always wondered if there wasn't something fishy about those two. Their background didn't lead to any warm fuzzy feelings. It turned out that before, during or after WWII, Willem and Greta "moved" to Argentina to live. They stayed there for almost 15 years and then immigrated to the United States. They never sought US citizenship and were very vague as to what they did or were educated in from their past. When they settled in the US, Greta did seamstress work out of her home and Willem became a janitor. Although from listening to him speak, he seemed to be highly educated and was at least quadra-lingual. Ellen darkly wondered if Greta used to make lamp shades out of human flesh but then got a check on her imagination and thought that that only happened in the movies, even though she knew from studying that there really were crazies from that war that did that sort of thing for fun. Willem could have been involved in anything to do with the war but Ellen and Daniel would never know because the Van Eyck's (or whoever they were) refused to talk about it.

Ellen struggled with the name of this new endeavor and one night at dinner, Ellen was asking the boys if they remembered any of the nursery rhymes they used to read when they were younger. The boys brought up several and reminisced about the plays that they would put on for their mom. This recollection was perfect.

So Ellen decided that she would write a book called, "<u>The Butcher, The Baker,</u> <u>The Evil Spy Maker</u>. She obviously changed the names and circumstances but she got the idea from the Van Eyck's. The first chapter of her new book was an explanation of how a couple who had been deviously, cunningly, and deceitfully involved in the Nazi movement and were instrumental in the workings of Hitler and Himmler, had snuck into our country and assumed the mild mannered identities of day laborers.

Ellen went on to describe the atrocities which were perpetrated by the cult-like members of Hitler's movement. When Ellen studied Hitler and his history in college with its horrendous consequences, she found it hard to believe that everyday people could be caught up in such meanness. It wasn't until she saw news broadcasts about mob violence in the 60's that she began to understand how someone might get carried away with the moment and with the crowd. But still that didn't excuse such violence to our fellow man.

Ellen decided to make her two main characters, Hans and Leisel, young doctors who were recruited by Himmler himself for their drive and membership in Hitler's youth organization. Hans and Leisel carried out horrific experiments on women and children before their subjects were "disposed of". And then in 1945, when their world got tossed upside down they quietly fled to Italy and through a distant cousin got on a boat to Africa which then transported them on to South America. After a few years when memories had faded, they moved into the US. There they became a silent contributor to the Nazi movement within the country. Their actions and deadly work finally caused them to be outed and then tried and executed. End of story.

In her preface for her new book and with the addition of the first chapter of the new endeavor with the second printing, the public had a good idea about what was to come. Ellen intended for her story to expose the members of this elite, wicked, and depraved community which had operated during Hitler's gruesome dirty work and which had used South America and other locations to hide their true identities and to continue on living their lives as if nothing had happened. She was researching with the local Jewish leaders and with a college professor who taught European history with an emphasis on WWII. She was having fun and feeling more alive than she had in a long time. And then things got weird

CHAPTER 7

ELLEN'S LIFE WAS humming along with a new sense of purpose and vigor. With the success of her first book and the creation of a new one, her life became more exciting and meaningful. The empty nest which was beginning to haunt her was taking on a fulfillment that the loss of the presence of her children had left. Ellen knew that when a woman spends twenty four hours a day, seven days a week fostering and helping and caring for her brood, it is an unnatural cessation of nurturing that happens almost overnight. She knew that the children, who had been the center of a woman's life, are gone out of her reach, out of the protective circle of her love, out of her attentive focus, leaves a void as big as the black hole. That void can never be totally filled. Ellen was no exception to this phenomenon. She loved the saying about motherhood and its ultimate outcome, "Motherhood is terminal". She often thought of that line when she would worry about something that was occurring to the boys' personal lives. Even though the older boys were no longer under her roof, the fretting and concern for their welfare and happiness were never out of her mind. There was not the immediacy which happens when they are pacing back and forth spilling out their feelings at the end of the day, which happened at the

Dinato household frequently, but there was a constancy that existed for all of them. The caring and closeness that they had for one another could never be extinguished. The Dinato's were a family and they were a good example of the adage that the family who played and prayed together stayed together. No matter what happened in the future, no matter where the boys lived, the unit of their family was forged like an unbreakable band of steel. There was a specific contentment that the whole family felt in that certainty. Ellen was sure of this and was gaining a new feeling of independence and freedom from her maternal duties but with a feeling that there was a loss of that 24/7 commitment. However, the success of her first book and the continued writing were helping to assuage those empty feelings. She had no idea however that her life was going to take on an unwanted direction and focus.

The doorbell rang one sunny afternoon shortly after the second printing of her book. And there stood two men in suits looking very governmental and serious. "Mrs. Dinato, Mrs. Ellen Dinato?, asked the taller gentleman.

"Yes", she said warily, "What can I do for you?"

"May we come in for a moment", asked the shorter one as he flashed his badge.

"Oh my God, what's happened?" "Are my children all right?" "Is my husband OK?" Her knees were shaking and the two men realized they had just scared this woman to death. A woman's worst nightmare is for the police to show up at their front door with deathly news.

"Oh, no, no, no, everything is fine", said the taller one, "We just have a few questions for you." And then the two showed Ellen their FBI identification and introduced themselves. The shorter, younger one with a head of unruly red hair was agent Michael Malone. The taller, older one was agent Jeff Portman and he seemed to be more in charge.

They actually had to lead Ellen into the living room because she was still shaking and placed her gently in a chair. "What do you mean, "questions". What could I possibly say that would interest the FBI?"

As they explained the situation to Ellen she started to settle down and her heart started to slow down. She reiterated, "Let me get this straight, you are here about my first book?" she asked incredulously.

"Yes," said agent Portman, "We want to know how you got the idea, how did you write this book?" They then congratulated her on her success but were curious as to how she came to write the book but were obviously evasive.

Ellen then regaled them about her dreams, her almost autobiographable descriptions, and her own personal details. When she finished, the two agents were staring at her in disbelief.

"Do you mean to tell me that you just cooked this up in your head?" asked agent Portman. "Or better yet in your dreams?" They both looked at her as if she were a fake clairvoyant and waited for her to tell another version.

"Really!" she said. "When I dream, I dream in whole scripts. I dream in color and my dreams are very lively and life like. I have read that our dreams are merely extensions of our conscious minds and that when we sleep our subconscious can create solutions to problems, answers to questions and, yes, even ideas for songs and books."

She looked at them as if they should totally comprehend what she was explaining but she could tell that they weren't really buying it. She continued to explain that she didn't know how else to convince them except that she could show them the rough draft, her notes, and the start of her next book which she was also inspired by a dream.

The two agents hesitated and then told her that that wouldn't be necessary. In a way, her explanation was so sincere and her responses so direct that after a few years of interrogating suspects in other areas, they knew when they were being lied to. And they concluded that Ellen was telling the truth. However, the dream part was hard to swallow for analytical thinkers. Then they asked her how she came up with the name of the "Illusive Crow". She again explained it was taking a nap again. And they just looked at each other. She further explained that as she was coming out of the fog of a relaxing sleep she faintly hears the cawing of the crows in their font meadow, and the name just popped into her head. She said, "You can even ask my friends and family who had to live through this whole book writing process. They can tell you even when I started having the dreams about these books."

Neither agent explained their visit, and they left abruptly. They politely thanked her for her time and were off to their sedan. Ellen was left with the weirdest feeling. Her heart was back to normal but her nervous system was flying high. "What on earth was that about?" she asked herself aloud.

When Daniel called that night from out-of-town, she told him about her encounter with the two agents. Daniel chastised her and asked her if she thought they were truly who they said they were. He was quite upset that she let two strange men in the house, especially living in such a secluded rural area. He told her if that ever happened again that she should get their names and numbers without opening the door and call to verify that they were who they said they were. He also told her that that is why the alarm system was right next to the front door and if she ever wondered about anyone that she should push the panic alarm. He also told her that that is what they paid the alarm company for every month so that he could have some peace of mind while he was away. Ellen was surprised at his fear and his anger but could understand both. She had always thought that the alarm system was for <u>her</u> peace of mind especially when she went to bed at night. After she would lull herself to sleep reading at night, the last thing she would do would be to sleepily look over and see if the red light, her safety beacon, was shining brightly and then she would close her eyes. She always slept soundly and knew that she and the boys were safe inside their home.

Ellen reassured Daniel that they were indeed who they said they were and had even left their cards. She had called the local FBI office and verified that they were indeed who they said they were. She even described them and the man on the other end of the line chuckled at her description. She was assured that agents Malone and Portman were indeed for real. Daniel felt much better and then apologized for jumping down her throat but he still made her promise if anybody showed up at their door that she wouldn't just whisk them in. He loved that open Midwestern part of Ellen but it scared him as well. After they each told each other about their day and about anything new within the last 24 hours, they said their good-nights and their "I love you's".

Daniel was always very thoughtful about calling every night. He said that if he had to be away from home, the least the company could do was to pay for a touch-base phone call every night. Ellen loved it because she didn't feel so alone – at least for just a few minutes each night. (Daniel traveled with a very haphazard schedule. Sometimes he was only gone two nights a week, sometimes all week. It was never the same. But it was part of the job.) She proceeded to check the locks of the house for the night, put on the alarm after their two dogs were brought back in after one last run around the yard, and turned off the lights as she walked her same walk through the house to end her day. Her youngest was asleep and beginning to lightly snore, but not nearly as loudly as Daniel. That must develop with age – like a fine old wine – getting better with age. But there was a certain comfort level at listening to them snore. She knew that they were at peace and sleeping deeply.

After the weekend and their speedy trip up to visit their two sons in college, Daniel was off again. It was now a ritual. Friday night, unpack, sort laundry, wash, dry and hopefully not press anything. And Sunday night, repack and get ready for another week. Now that Ellen and Daniel had only one left at home, the laundry was much easier to keep up with. When all the boys were home, Ellen usually did two to three loads a day – especially when they were playing sports. On weekends, Ellen had Daniel's to do and then any extra that she didn't get to. When they went up to see the boys in college, she had to hurriedly do Daniel's laundry Friday night but she could sleep on the way up on their three hour drive. Ellen and Daniel loved visiting and being a complete family again. They both knew that it wouldn't be long before the boys were out on their own, living who knows where, and having fewer visits. They also knew that when the boys married that it would get even more complicated because then they would have to share. Thanksgiving here, Christmas there. They didn't really want to think about it. They just wanted to enjoy having them near and having fun. And besides, Frankie missed his brothers.

Sonny, Danny and Frankie were all characters. Whenever the whole family got together, it wasn't quiet. There was usually so much laughter that they would get wicked looks from people at nearby tables in restaurants. Stewardesses would come over and ask the family to keep it down because there were other passengers who were trying to sleep. Where ever they went they had fun and it wasn't tranquil. Neither Ellen nor Daniel ever wanted to have riches. They were quite comfortable with what they had and only wanted their boys to have health, happiness and a good future. They didn't spend a lot of time orchestrating things for their sons because they were positive that their sons would succeed. Not only did they know that they were intelligent but more importantly they had very high EQs. All of the boys, even though each possessed their own identity and personality, had a great presence. They knew how to talk to anybody. And none of the boys were shy. They were always the leaders and not the followers. They were street smart and had experiences that a lot of their classmates didn't have. Rather than have expensive toys like some of their friends, the Dinato family traveled. And having moved so much and having faced so many new experiences prepared them to think on their feet – a valuable trait.

With fun memories of the last weekend still swirling in her head, Ellen walked down their driveway to the mailbox. The Dinato's lived on eleven acres of woods. The driveway was two acres long and wound around so that no one could see the house from the road. Daniel and Ellen liked the idea of the privacy, but with the seclusion came the added burden that they couldn't see the end of the driveway. As an end result, Ellen, who had had a kidnapping scare when she was eight, insisted on driving the boys down to the end of the driveway to catch the school bus. God forbid, if anyone had taken one of the boys, Ellen would never have known who or what or why. So she religiously drove them down. Now that Frankie could drive, she didn't have to worry about going in all kinds of weather. But today was beautiful. The Adirondack mountain air was whisking through the trees and she felt invigorated walking down the stone path. When she reached the mail box she noticed that it was slightly ajar. This was unusual because the mailman always put down the flag and tightly secured the box lid. People in the country know that to leave the box lid open can invite unwanted visitors. It was bad enough that wasps, bees and ants felt free to visit, but there could be other things as well. As she opened the box she was appalled at what she saw. There was a dead crow with its head severed. At first she thought it might be a practical joke like the time the neighbor kids stuck their banana peels in the mailbox. But then she saw that the crow had been purposely mangled. She picked up a stick and drug it out of the box and let it drop on the ground. There, attached to a wing was a note which had been produced by cutting capital letters out of a newspaper or a magazine. Big, bold letters, spelled out, "STOP WRITING". Gradually fear replaced question and she knew it was a threat – but from whom? She pushed the crow into the gully hoping that a nocturnal carrion eater would help itself to what was left of the crow and slowly walked up the drive.

When Daniel called that night she recanted her tale of the dead crow and he was silent. Finally he asked if she had called the police. The police where they lived consisted of town constables. These constables were not trained law officers but were community citizens who offered for a very small salary to patrol the areas roads. They were given official patrol cars and were armed but they had not been given extensive training on public safety. She told Daniel that she had indeed called the town constable and that he had come out right away. He looked at the crow and told her that even though it was a federal offense because they had misused a federal mailbox, he couldn't "make heads or tails" out of this message. He cajoled Ellen and treated her like a pouting child and reassured her that it was probably somebody's twisted idea of a joke. He asked if she knew of any one who was jealous of her newly found fame. For a moment she was silent and then just shook her head and told him that she had only well wishers and congratulations from everyone. When she finished telling Daniel about this episode he concurred with the constable. He agreed that it was probably somebody's stupid attempt at humor. But Ellen heard the uncertainty in Daniel's voice. She wanted him to feel better so she told him that he was probably right and went on with the rest of her conversation. But she went to bed that night totally puzzled.

First there was a visit from the FBI and now this. She was beginning to think that maybe being a dull housewife wasn't so bad after all.

The next day Ellen had to make her bi-weekly trip to the grocery. Since Sonny and Danny were in college she only had to go to the grocery store twice a week and now she could usually get away with just one cart. Even though Ellen had only one son at home, food disappeared like a vanishing species. It used to be a two cart experience and at one Christmas time, after Ellen finished filling the first cart with groceries she pushed it up above the checkout line to prepare to fill the second. Since it was the holiday, the store had their usual cart at the very front of the store for proceeds to the poor. The lady in the next aisle spotted Ellen's first loaded cart and walked over and placed three cans of food in her cart. Ellen saw what the lady was doing and was touched and tickled at the same time. "Oh, no, I'm sorry but that is not the cart for the poor, it's my cart." The lady blushed and was embarrassed. To keep her from feeling upset, Ellen then joked and said, "Well, hey, maybe I should have kept my mouth shut – I can use all the help I can get feeding my brood." It made everyone around her laugh and the tension was broken. Ellen was very good at that. Her friends called her the peacemaker. Ellen was the one people called upon to help mediate and to advocate in several situations in the community. She just had that way about her.

After she had paid at the counter and ushered her cart outside she looked for where she had parked her car. With her lone grocery cart loaded to the brim Ellen started walking. As she left the protected sidewalk of the shopping center, she edged into the lane of traffic. She quickly looked both ways and started across the lanes. Out of the corner of her eye she spotted a fleeting dark shadow. From out of nowhere a navy blue late model car with tinted windows was roaring down at her. Ellen only had time to jerk back but the grocery cart didn't fare as well. The car smashed into the side of the cart and hurled it over on its side almost hitting a lady and her child trying to enter the store. As quickly as it had appeared, it screamed past and left through the farthest exit. There was no time for a license number or even a description of the driver

If she hadn't noticed, she would have been smashed as quickly as her grocery cart. Instead she stood still. Ellen didn't know if the scream she heard was hers or from someone else but she just stood there in shock. Immediately onlookers came rushing up and asked her if she was OK. She didn't answer but just stared at what could have been her on the pavement. People up righted her cart and started to place the groceries back in. The bread was smashed into mush and the eggs broke but everything else seemed to have survived albeit with some dents and marks.

When the store manger came out to inquire what on earth had happened Ellen just shakily explained that someone apparently hadn't seen her or her cart and just went roaring by. The dark blue car with tinted windows didn't allow her or anyone else to see who was driving. But she knew that there would be a mark on the car because there was some fresh looking navy blue paint on the metal side of the cart and that was the color of the car. That seemed to be too much for a coincidence. The manager said that the driver had to have been going awfully fast for them to knock the cart over and to leave paint on the cart. He also told her that they had had several close calls where speeding teenagers roaring through the parking lot like they were on the Daytona 500 track. He apologized and Ellen said that it was alright and no harm was done, but she silently wondered if it really had been a speeding teenager or someone else with a different motive. Perhaps it was the person telling her to stop writing and wanted to frighten her – or worse. Again she ignored her natural instinct for survival and chastised herself for having such a lively imagination.

The only injury Ellen had was a sore wrist from the cart being ripped from her grip. The manager offered to have Ellen come into the store and sit down and even call the EMT's, but she insisted on just going home. She had had enough excitement for one day. She didn't even tell Daniel that night because she didn't want him to worry. She could tell him Wednesday when he flew home.

On Thursday, she looked for the card of the FBI agents. After she told Daniel about the weird things that had happened to her, he told her that she should call the county police just to inform them of these strange happenings. But Ellen didn't know anyone from the county sheriff's department but she did know someone at the FBI. Since the mailbox, a federal property, had been used in a threat, she felt like she had an excuse to call them more than the locals. Besides, she didn't have as much confidence in the locals because they didn't seem to be as accomplished and learned as the federal agents.

Having found Agent Portman's card, she called his office. He answered after the second ring and was surprised to hear from Ellen. She sheepishly explained the reason for her call and waited for the agent to respond. There was a pregnant pause. Then he told her that the events were definitely out of the ordinary and he told her that he could come out and check out her story. There wasn't anything pressing that the agent was working on and so he could take this courtesy time to visit Ellen and see what was going on for himself.

When Ellen opened the door for Agent Portman, she once again let him right in. She was silently laughing to herself about letting a strange man in when her husband wasn't home but realized as isolated as they were the neighbors couldn't gossip or start rumors when they couldn't see a thing. Agent Portman had called ahead to tell of his arrival time and Ellen had made coffee and set out slices of her famous banana nut bread. They casually sat in the kitchen and the agent felt the warmth of this home and enjoyed the scents of a well used kitchen.

Ellen started out by asking him if she should call him Agent Portman or Mr. Portman and he chuckled and said that he wasn't in his office so she should just call him Jeff. This wasn't a true official call so he felt comfortable telling her that. He also complimented her on such rich tasting coffee and her great bread. It had been years since he had been in a home that so reminded him of the home of his youth. The smells, the welcoming feel, it was just automatically cozy and welcoming. He envied the Dinato family for their comfort.

Ellen proceeded to reiterate the events of the last few days and asked him what he thought. Jeff told her that it really could be just two weird incidents that were not related. The dead crow could have been someone's sick sense of humor and envy and the grocery cart could have been a simple accident. Ellen listened and told him that that was exactly what her husband had said. She felt better but didn't realize that Jeff was seriously considering that they were on purpose and could be related. If that were the case, then he knew that this was probably not going to end but indeed to escalate. Ellen also felt a little silly but she took it upon herself to tell Jeff whom she had crafted her second book after. She told all about the weird family who she thought were indeed German and were the right ages to have had something to do with WWII. He wrote down the information and waited.

As Ellen was pouring him a second cup of coffee, Jeff was looking around at her home. Jeff asked if she had had a decorator do her home and she just laughed and told him that decorating and arranging were her hobby. He couldn't get over the hominess and the feeling of warmth that surrounded him. The family room which was incorporated into the large eat-in kitchen was quite expansive. The focal point was an entire wall of antique brick with a colonial fireplace in the center. The mantle was a giant aged beam which had come from the barn on the land on which the home was built. It was a sin to destroy an historic barn but the wood and beams had been put to good use. Some of the barn wood Ellen had been able to use to frame a large quilt above the couch. It all looked like something from a magazine. Jeff became silent for a moment and Ellen noticed that he was somewhere else in thought. She patiently waited for him to come back from his reverie and then asked him if he were interested in antiques. Wanting to postpone leaving, Jeff assured Ellen that he was. She took him on a tour of their home and pointed out certain pieces which had been passed down to her from her Amish ancestors. She was specifically proud of her Grandmother's side-ways butter churn and her lard press which she had artistically used to display dried flowers. Everywhere he looked he saw signs of a happy family. There were family photos of three grinning imps at varios stages of growth, antiqued toys which looked as if the family really did use them, and a comfort that was all encompassing. He felt that he could stay forever but he knew he had to get back to the office. Jeff assured Ellen that she could call him any time if there were any other things that came up. He secretly wished that there would be a reason to revisit and enjoy this home and this refreshing lady but he certainly didn't wish her or her family harm.

Ellen's life was now becoming a mix of intrigue and excitement. The more people talked about her book and the more exposure she got from the community and surrounding area, the more her name appeared in the paper. She was asked to do a book signing at the small book store in the town where her sons attended high school. The local and area papers took publicity shots and the library where she had spent many a frenzied hour helping her sons research for papers had asked her to do a book reading from her new book. They asked her to whet their appetites for the latest book. All of this commotion had its down side. Whoever didn't want her to continue writing was still out there.

Two days after Agent Portman visited the Dinato household, Ellen received a threatening letter. Once again it was cut up letters on simple white paper and it told her, "Stop writing or else". She didn't hesitate this time to make her call to the FBI. Ellen called Jeff Portman who was out of his office but she left a message on his voice mail. She told him about the latest contact with this weird person or persons and she also told him that it did fall under the federal jurisdiction because the person or persons had used the United States Postal Service. By sending something through the mail, he/she/ or they had broken the law, especially with a threat attached. This was getting to be too much. She also called the local constable and filled him in on the latest comings and goings but he just brushed it off as some weirdo trying to get her attention. Having lived here for several years, she was amazed that anything was happening to her in such a benign area of the country. Nothing ever happened out here. Or so she thought.

When Jeff returned to his office he played his messages and listened to Ellen's message with interest. Her voice was strong and confident but he could also pick up a certain amount of fright and puzzlement. He immediately called her and asked if he could come out and pick up the letter and have it analyzed. She assured him that that would be fine and was relieved to know that another adult would be in the house for a little while because Daniel was out of town. It did get lonely when Daniel was gone and it was nice to know that she could talk to someone else besides the squirrels that scampered to the bird feeders which were continually having to be refilled. Young Danny wasn't home very much because it was his senior year and he not only had school, but an after school job and his plentiful socializing. And besides, she didn't want to scare him but she did warn him to be watchful for anything out of the ordinary. As a typical teenager he thought his mother had blown all of this out of proportion and was being overdramatic and worrying way too much. But even though he thought it was humorous, he also secretly wondered if this could be a real threat.

Jeff once again was ushered into the Dinato home and this time he smelled the aroma of homemade sauce. He took in the aroma of garlic, onion and olive oil intermingling with crushed tomatoes. This time Ellen served coffee in the family room in front of the fire. She had just taken some sugar cookies out of the oven before he arrived. They both sat in front of the fire and talked about the latest incident. She handed him the letter and envelope that she had placed in a plastic baggy. She showed him that the letter had been addressed specifically to her and had a local postmark She knew from watching television that she had handled the letter and that her prints would be on it. She also told him that her prints were already on file with the government because she had been a GS-9 with the Department of Defense. So any other prints that were found were from whom sent the letter.

Jeff made a pig of himself with the cookies and enjoyed the camaraderie and the conversation. Unfortunately Jeff had had the start of a family when he married twenty one years ago. His marriage lasted seven years and then it was just over. His wife, Maggie, had put off having children because he was just getting started in her career as a social worker. She loved her job and was involved with children all day long. This seemed to appease her ticking clock and she knew that with Jeff's commitment to the FBI that they would be moving periodically and that their time together would be limited. Jeff's hours were atrocious and she could be called out at a moment's notice. So after seven years the words "until death do us part" disintegrated and Jeff found an apartment and started his solitary life. At first Jeff poured all of his heart into the job. But as time slipped by, he was haunted by the possible memory of a family and of children and of growing old with someone. It wasn't easy because he had no one to vent to. He couldn't share his feelings, his concerns or even his day with someone else. Each night he came home to a dark apartment which echoed of his loneliness. He didn't even have a pet because his hours were so bizarre that it was not conducive to taking care of something else. He was definitely a dog person and that was out of the question. So he accepted his solitary life and tried to fill it with work. That is why he had succeeded as much as he had. He was definitely a dedicated government man. The quandary he was having was that soon he would be up for retirement and he had no clue as to what he would do from there. He had had some friends who just merely retired and enjoyed their pension, while others went off and started new careers. He had a few years yet and he would always postpone seriously thinking about it until a time when he was in a better frame of mind – whenever that would be.

In the fourteen years that he had been divorced, he had dated several people but had never found someone who he could love as much as Maggie. Jeff had been devastated that his marriage had ended. And the dating scene now was so different than when he was in college that he thought he was living in the wrong century. Women today were much more forward and aggressive. To an old-fashioned guy it was a good boost for his ego but these women (not ladies) were not the marrying type. He was baffled as to why so many women wanted to shuck the domestic life for a life of parties, parties, parties or career. career, career. They seemed to be "Me" oriented and that was a true turnoff for him. He longed for a woman who could make a good home full of love and caring and domestic bliss. He had given up finding such a woman and just enjoyed his occasional roll in the hay.

As he sat by the fire he mused to himself, "Now this is the kind of woman I am looking for". He hadn't felt so comfortable in another woman's presence since Maggie. And she would have to be married. "Damn", he thought, "just my luck".

After talking about anything and everything, they knew that the afternoon visit was over. Both reluctantly said good-bye and Jeff left to return to the office.

One thing that stuck in Ellen's mind after he left was how would this person or persons who were threatening her know that she would or wouldn't stop writing? He or they could threaten but how would they know to stop and then a chilling thought hit her. Since she lived out in the middle of nowhere they did not have curtains on the windows. They had no neighbors and the only time they used the room darkening shades was at night when they went to bed. Daily she would write at the computer which was in the guest wing of their home. The guest room served as a bedroom for visitors and an office with the computer and everything that one could use to write. And the guest room/office had no curtains. She rushed into the office and stared out the window looking for any movement and all she saw were trees, trees, and more trees. The dogs would bark if any one came any where near their yard but this was a periodic event. Deer, raccoons, squirrels, wild turkeys, snakes, would all set the dogs off. They had such good hearing that they could hear things that Ellen couldn't possibly hear. She wondered if the dogs had been barking more recently but she couldn't remember anything out of the ordinary. She immediately pulled down the shades and stood there and shook. She felt so violated and she didn't even know for sure if anyone had been on her property. But she also knew that she wrote with the lights on in the office and even that couldn't be hidden from anybody on the outside. This was getting to be too much. Then she felt a little silly and she knew that her boys and her husband would really give her a hard time and tell her that she had been watching too much television or reading too many thrillers.

Two days later, another letter arrived.

The letter was once again cut out letters on common

white paper – same nondescript envelope – and this time it said, "If you don't stop writing someone will die!" That was it. She was instantly nauseated and her heart was up in her throat. She wasn't thinking of herself. She thought she could take care of herself but when someone was threatening her family – that was the last straw. The first thing she did was to call Agent Portman and then she sat down and cried. She had been fine up to this point because it all seemed so nebulous. But now this changed everything. Jeff arrived an hour later with Agent Malone in tow. This time they not only took the letter and envelope in the baggy from her but they searched outside along the perimeter of her home. Since it was daylight and there was a skiff of snow on the ground they could easily tell the difference between animal prints and humans. Sure enough there were men's tracks leading up to a stand of cedars nearest the office window. These trees were at least fifty feet from the house but since they never lost their needles they served as a nice blind for anyone who wanted to peer in unnoticed. There were no cigarette butts or candy wrappers or anything so the person apparently hadn't been there too long. It was getting very chilly out. It was mid-fall and any day heavy snow could fall. It was not an ideal situation to be sitting out in the woods. But there indeed had been someone close to the Dinato house. When they went back in they told her that they had found some tracks and asked if any of the boys had been out in the woods recently. Ellen knew that they had not because the older two were away in school and Danny had not had time to just take off in the woods. And her husband was off on business. Since it had snowed just last night and early this morning, they knew that the tracks were fresh.

Now both men became more serious and business like. They told her that they would confer with the local authorities and ask them to watch and patrol the house from the road. In addition, they told her that she should also keep her eyes out for anything out of the ordinary. It was very conspicuous to see a car parked on the side of the rode and several times she had stopped to question why people were there. Most often the people were water testing personnel who were testing the land for wells as the farmers slowly sold off their land for future building. The road the Dinato's lived on was a mile and a half long and had 33 families living on it. The town had strict building codes and the lots had to be at least 5 acre parcels in order to build. It was a friendly road with neighbors pitching in when there was a crisis but other than that, the Dinato's rarely saw any one because it wasn't a true neighborhood. It was the country. There also were very few cars on the road. With the exception of "rush hour", there were more squirrels on the road than cars. It was unusual to see more than one car every ten or fifteen minutes. So it was easy to tell if a strange new car was going down the road.

The agents then told Ellen that the first envelope and letter proved to be a dead-end. There were no prints on either except for Ellen's and that left them nowhere. The paper and envelope could have been purchased from any number of local stores.

Both agents explained that they too would be watchful and that they would be in touch with her. Anytime there was a death threat the agents took it seriously. They returned to the office with the copy of the first book autographed personally by Ellen. It contained the first chapter of the next book and they were going to read it and see what was in it that could possibly make someone angry enough to want Ellen to stop writing.

That night Jeff went home to a frozen dinner even though he knew how to cook. This night he wanted to put some thought into this new case. He arranged his dinner on his collapsible TV tray and settled into his favorite leather winged back chair and ate while he read. As he finished the first chapter of the new book his dinner sat there half eaten and distastefully cold. He was starting to get an idea of just who might be enraged with this book when the phone rang and jerked him out of his thoughts. It was Ellen and she was hysterical. She could hear Frankie in the background trying to calm her down but she was inconsolable. "They killed them, they killed them", she sobbed. "Killed whom?", Jeff asked. "My dogs", she cried. "I went out to bring them in for the night and they didn't come when I called. That was very unusual because they were usually very eager to come in and be with the family. I went out looking for them when I didn't hear or see them and I found them lying there like they had been in horrible pain but they didn't move. They may have been poisoned because they had foamed at the mouth." Both dogs, Copper and Duchess, were mixed breeds and had almost an acre of land to run. They both wore the <u>Invisible Fence</u> collars and were always running after anything and everything in the back yard. They were an integral part of the family. The boys were raised with the dogs and were very close. The whole family even had their Christmas pictures taken each year with Copper and Duchess. They were all in the family. With Daniel traveling so much the dogs gave the boys something else to bond to when their father wasn't in the home. It was a very healthy relationship. And now they were both dead.

Jeff said he would be right there. He didn't call his partner Malone. He decided to let him have his alone time with his new bride and handle this himself. He would fill him in on this tomorrow. When Jeff arrived he found Ellen tear streaked but calmer. Her eyes were swollen and puffy from crying. Frankie, her youngest son, answered the door with his mother. There was no mistaking him as her son. He had the same coloring as his mom and they were built the same. He didn't seem to have inherited much of the Italian blood from his father but he could tell that there was a mix of them both from having seen family photos. They walked into the kitchen and sat at the family table. Frankie was quite subdued and Jeff could tell that Frankie had been crying too. Nothing like this had ever happened to their family and Ellen and Frankie just sat there catatonically and stared at Jeff as if he were going to be able to go out in the back yard and raise them from the dead. Jeff didn't have any answers but he would do something to help. Jeff had already called the local sheriff's department and they said that they would dispatch a county highway worker to pick up the dogs and take them to the Dinato's vet to be examined. But from the description Ellen gave him, he was pretty sure that the dogs had indeed been poisoned. Just then there were lights coming up the driveway and Jeff went out to greet the highway department worker. Jeff asked that Ellen and

Frankie stay in the house, but they insisted on saying goodbye to their family pets. Of course this brought on new tears and when they were finished with their last time with Copper and Duchess, they walked back into their house. Again they sat at the kitchen table.

By now, Jeff knew that this had escalated and that whoever was trying to scare Ellen was succeeding. Now there had been a true crime committed. Killing someone's defenseless pets was a cowardly, vengeful act. And he knew that if they could cold-heartedly kill pets that there wasn't much of stretch to think that this person could go even further. However, he didn't want to upset either Frankie or Ellen by being blunt so he told them that just out of precaution they should use their alarm 24 hours a day and not just when they went to bed. Jeff also told them that he didn't want either of them to make any superfluous trips anywhere and to try to stay close to home. Frankie asked if he should stay home from school and protect his mom but Jeff said that the arrangement should be that life goes on as usual and that they should just be very aware of their surroundings. As they were talking, the phone rang and it was Daniel. Again the tears were flowing and Ellen had to recount the tragic event. Ellen told her husband that Agent Portman was there and that seemed to calm him down. Daniel reassured his wife that he would be home tomorrow night and that he would look into curtailing his traveling until this situation calmed down. Needless to say no one slept well that night. Ellen kept listening for any sounds and slept fitfully when she finally fell asleep. Daniel was in a strange bed in a hotel and just wanted to be home. And Frankie lay in bed for hours mourning the loss of his two beloved dogs. He finally slept and dreamt of people chasing him out in the woods with poison bottles in their hands.

Jeff went home to his apartment and called the Dinato's vet. There was always someone on duty until late in the evening in this practice of eight vets. The vet told Jeff that it did look like the dogs were poisoned and that he was sending a tox screen to the state for analysis. He also said that when they were finished that he would have the dogs cremated and the ashes returned to the Dinato's. Jeff thanked him and tried to go to sleep. He had not informed Ellen of his suspicions but would tomorrow. She had enough on her plate at this moment. Tomorrow was soon enough.

The next day was brisk but not snowing. Jeff had arranged to come out to the Dinato's at nine. Ellen looked haggard but was trying to keep up a brave front. She welcomed Jeff in and they went into the family room. She asked him if he would like coffee and he told her that he had just recently had breakfast and maybe he would take her up on it later. He started chatting about her new book and asked her how she got started on this new topic. Once again Ellen told him that it had come to her in a dream. This time the topic – the Nazis – was something that Ellen had had to study in school. She even had gone to Dachua when they lived in Germany and had seen first hand what a concentration camp had looked like. It was a very disturbing and haunting visit. Those scenes and the photographs of the living conditions were something that could not be erased from one's memory. She also told Jeff about her run-ins with her sister-in-law's parents and how mystifying that had been. She discounted them because the mother had died and the father was very old. Ellen could tell what Jeff was hinting at. She apparently had stirred up a hornet's nest with her research and writing about the Nazis. She had wondered about that too but had dismissed the idea because she knew no one else who could possibly have anything to do with this. She thought it definitely had to be a stranger. So she had no leads, no place to suggest to look.

Jeff knew that he would contact the other FBI agents in his office who worked with subversive groups and kept track of trouble makers and people who made threats. Unfortunately there was always a mass of people, malcontents, mentally ill, who let the world know about their grievances. There were religious cults, right wing extremists, survivalists and all kinds of people who were unhappy with just about everybody. And he knew that the Nazi party and its followers were still alive and well and feeding off of these vulnerable malcontents who hadn't found their niche in society. They were not just in Germany but all over the world. Some were closet members and others were totally out there recruiting. If one looked deeply enough it was shocking as to how many there were out there. The average American had no idea of the number of twisted people they lived around. Jeff knew that was just as well.

He left Ellen with the same instructions that he had given her the preceding evening. Use the alarm, no unnecessary trips anywhere, and be hyper-vigilant. He told her to close the electric garage door the instant she pulled into the garage and before she got out of the car. Ellen reassured him that she did those things any way. Now that she didn't have the dogs to warn her any more, she had only the alarm for protection. But she knew that Daniel would fly in tonight. They parted uneasily and Jeff had more work to do.

Two days later, Ellen had to go to the grocery store again. It was not only the three people in the household to feed, but the boys always had extra kids with them and she never knew how many people were actually going to be seated at the dinner table each night. And Danny was no exception. Now that the older boys weren't home, Frankie liked to have extra people over to keep him company and Ellen couldn't blame him. Ellen missed the noise and commotion as much as Frankie and Daniel did. She always went with a small list and ended up with an overflowing cart. Groceries were a necessary trip and so she set off to get food for the next two or three days.

As she was returning from her shopping jaunt she turned onto her country road. Up ahead she could see flashing lights and emergency vehicles parked in the road. As she slowly crept past the vehicles she noticed a Chevy Suburban overturned in the gully. In fact it was identical to hers and she recognized her neighbor, Jessica Newman, as the driver. Both women owned the same kind and color of car and often joked when they parked near each other at school and sporting events. They said that some day they would end up trying to get into each others cars and then they would really be embarrassed.

She rolled her window down and asked the aging volunteer fireman what had happened. The fireman answered that someone in a dark blue car had forced Jessica off the road. He told her that even though they had to use the "Jaws of Life", that Jessica was conscious and talking. She was bruised and scraped and very shaken up but her seatbelt and the fact that her car was built like a tank helped keep her from further serious injury. They were definitely taking her to the hospital but he said that the EMT's were pretty sure that she would be OK.

Ellen was totally numb. "That does it!" said Ellen to herself. "This is just too bizarre!" Whenever Ellen was stressed she would feel as if she were having an out-of-body experience. Her subconscious would take hold of her movements and help her maintain what ever she needed to do. She drove the rest of the way home and very quickly put her car in the garage and immediately put down the door. She sat for a minute getting her thoughts straight and decided that she would try to calmly call Jeff. Hopefully he would tell her that her imagination was running rampant and that it was all just coincidence, but she knew better. She knew instinctively that this was way off the scale of just circumstance. But she knew that she had to report this latest incident and see what Jeff would say and do. Because Jeff was in town and Daniel was off on business again, at a trip that was very important to his company, she felt relieved that a man could actually be there for them. It always seemed that Daniel was out of town when there was a crisis. Ellen got quite good at repairing and trouble shooting and taking the bull by the horns, but this was different. For so many years Ellen had played the strong "I can handle anything that comes along" role that she was used to the stiff upper lip. But this was above and beyond the ordinary and now she was actually afraid. She was afraid for her children, her husband and herself. And now she had even endangered her neighbor. She never dreamt that writing a book could backfire so drastically and actually be a cause for concern for their very safety. She would rather die than have anything happen to her family. She was feeling quite guilty when she called Jeff. And he promised to come right out.

When Jeff arrived Frankie had just arrived home from school and was changing to go to his job. Jeff was glad he caught him because after the description of this afternoon's incident, Jeff didn't want any of them taking any unnecessary trips. He informed Frankie that as of now that he was not to go to his job. "Oh my God, complained Frankie, "I'll get fired". Jeff reassured Frankie that he would talk to his boss and set him straight as to why he wouldn't be in to work for the next week or so. Frankie felt relieved and was glad that an actual FBI agent was going to run interference for him at his job. He secretly hoped that Jeff would ask him to stay home from school, too, but no such luck. But it was his senior year and he was going through senioritis and was doing more playing than studying anyway. Ellen looked at Frankie and felt awful about what she was putting her son through. She was relieved to see Frankie bounce back with his usual youthful exuberance and acceptance. Jeff then recommended that Frankie leave his car at home for a week or two and ride the bus to and from school. That is a sentence worse than death to a senior but he took it maturely and began to understand that this was really serious and that these adults were taking every precaution to keep the Dinato family safe. Jeff made a hurried call to Frankie's boss and the man very generously understood. He told Jeff to tell Frankie that he could come back when he could and his job would still be there. Jeff didn't know if the man was truly sincere or half afraid of butting heads with the FBI.

When Frankie left to go to his room and get a head start on his homework, Ellen invited Jeff to join her in the kitchen. She was fixing chicken piccata, polenta and greens for dinner and asked Jeff if he wanted to stay. She assured him that they had plenty and she always cooked enough for an army. Jeff quickly accepted and marveled at how at ease he felt here in this house. Ellen was busying herself at the stove and she recounted the neighbor's incident. She explained about the identical cars and the fact that she and Jessica even resembled each other. They had the same color hair and were approximately the same size. It was beginning to sink in that she had inadvertently caused her neighbor to be injured. If it had been one half hour earlier, it would have probably been Ellen who was being rushed to the hospital.

Jeff sat for a moment after she was finished and thought out what he was going to say next. He wanted to choose his words carefully so that he wouldn't alarm Ellen more than she was. He didn't want to make light of the incident because Ellen might think that he wasn't taking all of this seriously. He was quite serious and knew that this was all an attempt to scare her which was working. "Ellen", he said softly, "I want you to know that we are taking this whole threatening situation for what it is and what it could be. For the time being, I want you to stay close to home and keep the house alarmed at all times. In addition to Frankie just going to school and back, I want you to ask a friend to do your grocery shopping for you and deliver them here. It is good that you can see and hear who is coming up the driveway. Without the dogs now, I want you to be hyper vigilant as to who is around your home. Do not invite anyone to deliver anything that is not entirely necessary and do not open the door unless you absolutely know them intimately. We do not know what this person or persons intends or what their real purpose is. Or even if it is a "he" or a "she".

"Oh, you don't think that I did these things, do you?" she gasped. Jeff looked at her in puzzlement and asked her, "What on earth made you ask that? There is no way after visiting you and your family that we would think that you are capable of doing something as insidious as this, just to get publicity for your books. Don't worry, we crossed that off our list soon after we met you." Ellen looked distressed. Jeff stood up and walked over to her. "I'm serious. There is no way that you are on our suspect list." He placed his hand gently on her shoulder and he could see the wear on her from the last few days had placed on her. Tears ran down her cheeks and she wiped her face with her sleeve. "I'm sorry, Jeff. It is just that this is so out of the norm for me. I'm just a simple housewife and I 'm not used to this kind of intrigue and commotion." She straightened herself and gained control and continued explaining. "I wrote these books to get out of the rut I was in. With the children leaving and Daniel gone so much, I was floundering to find something meaningful to do." Jeff patted her shoulder and told her that she wasn't <u>just</u>

a housewife. He said it was ludicrous to ever describe herself as such. He told her that she had many talents and was a breath of fresh air from the people he usually had to deal with. He enlightened her that any man would be proud to have such a multi-talented and caring spouse. He went on to explain that too many women in this generation put too much emphasis on getting ahead and gleaning monetarily, placing their physical shape above child rearing and nurturing. He expressed his acceptance of a woman who would put her family first and would care so much about their individual happiness. He was looking into her eyes and she could feel the warmth of his closeness. He also told her that they would get to the bottom of this whole unfortunate situation and things would get back to normal. Jeff knew when he said those words that when this ended, he wouldn't be able to come out here and visit at the drop of a hat. He would have no excuse and this saddened him.

Ellen blushed. She hadn't been talked to like this in years. One time she remembered a fellow teacher in Germany taking Daniel aside and telling him how lucky he was to be marrying her. She overheard this comment and beamed with pride. She knew that deep down inside that Daniel was indeed proud of her and was appreciative of the many things she did for the family. But with work being his mistress, Daniel too often forgot to tell Ellen exactly how he felt. As in so many marriages there was a certain level of silent knowledge that your spouse is to understand exactly how you feel. But, was it nice to hear things like this now and then. Ellen was speechless. She was embarrassed at this kind of unusual attention and didn't know what to say next. She decided to break the ice by moving away from him and offering him some wine before dinner. He accepted and they continued chatting about the dinner and how she prepared it. They didn't get back on the topic of her stalker until dinner was finished.

Jeff offered to help with the dishes and Ellen laughed. She said that hers was a one person kitchen until the boys got home and then she had to take the back seat to their creations. All three boys had turned into quite accomplished cooks. They weren't chef quality yet but they were on the road to being great catches for any woman. She told Jeff that the two older boys had dinner together every Sunday night at college and the boys in Sonny's apartment had gotten together with the girls next door and would have Sunday night cook-offs. They would call home at least once a month to ask for some recipe from their home and Ellen was thrilled. Jeff marveled at how Ellen's eyes lit up when she talked about any of her children. He could tell that she was totally dedicated to them and that theirs was a closeness that not many families had. He listened quietly as she told him about some of their early fiascos in the kitchen. They had even used their Lite Bright set to make the name of an Italian restaurant and the boys would create their own menu and serve dinner to Daniel and Ellen. They would put on pressed white shirts and black ties and throw a white napkin across their wrists and pretend to be the waiters. Breakfast in bed on Saturday mornings was their specialty. Ellen told him about one morning of waking up to the usual crash, bang, boom and high voices which hadn't entered puberty yet, creating in the kitchen. Both Daniel and Ellen smelled an unusual odor and were trying to guess what concoction they had come up with. When the boys were done with their creations and had delivered breakfast in bed, both Daniel and Ellen would go down to see what was left of their kitchen and laugh at the scene of destruction. This particular morning Sonny was carrying a heavy tray laden with some scrambled eggs and toast. He excitedly placed the tray between his parents and then asked the question that Ellen so often would ask at the table, "Guess what is in it?" By asking what the tastes were and the ingredients Ellen had taught the boys about herbs and vegetables, meats and produce, and varying cooking techniques. This way they knew a lot about food before most kids learned how to cook. Both Ellen and Daniel stared at the eggs and couldn't figure out what was different. The smell was most unusual. Sonny broke the silence and informed them that he had been watching a cooking show on TV after school one day and James Beard was offering his recipe for a liqueur omelet. So, Sonny decided to make one this Saturday morning. He went searching in the liquor cabinet and didn't quite know what liqueur was, so he just used a bottle of Jim Beam. Ellen and Daniel tried valiantly not to laugh and ate the "creation" very gingerly. It had been a family joke ever since.

Before Jeff knew it the evening had sped by. He didn't know when he had had such a good time. He was comfortable, well fed, entertained and felt totally at home. He could get used to this. He dreaded going back to his quiet, lonely apartment. Even though it had all the conveniences that a bachelor would want, it still seemed empty. There was no familiar laughter and the sharing of inside stories; no one to laugh at your jokes; no one to fix you your favorite meal and bake you a cake on your birthday. Yes, he could get used to this. When he left he promised Ellen that he would come back out tomorrow after work to check on everyone unless he was needed before then.

As he left the driveway he noticed a dark car creeping past on the road and suddenly sped up. He probably wouldn't have paid as much attention to this if the car's driver hadn't acted suspiciously. Instantly he wondered if this could be the stalker. Since he was headed in the wrong direction he had to find a driveway to turn around. The narrow two-laned country road at night was pitch black with no street lights to help a person along the way. When Jeff got turned around he went flying down the road to try to catch up with the car. Either the car had ducked into a driveway with his lights off or he had really gotten ahead of him. He wasn't at the end of the road which intersected the highway. Without any lights it was a lost cause. He pulled a u-turn and headed back toward the Dinato's. No one would ever imagine anything sinister happening out here. It was so peaceful, so bucolic. Even in the dark he could see the outlines in the moonlight of the forests, the empty fields glistening with a covering of snow, the occasional openings for driveways. As he drove home he thought about what the stalker's next move would be. He worried about the whole Dinato family. He was mystified as to why the stalker hadn't contacted Ellen by phone. Did he have an unmistakable voice or accent? Did Ellen already know his voice? It is part of an agent's training to try to get in the head of a criminal, try to think as he would think, and to try to profile the behavior and the traits from what little they had to go on.

This wasn't New York City. This was an historic settlement on the outskirts of the capital. It was small and close-knit and to some tediously boring. But it was the kind of community which was perfect for raising children. Jeff imagined that that was what had appealed to Ellen and Daniel to move here. The children here were not especially street smart but they knew how to help a neighbor and they knew what their values were. There wasn't much for them to do on weekends, so families would take turns and take it upon themselves to entertain the kids. They could skate, ski, snowmobile or ice fish during the winter months and several families had built large fire pits for the bonfires during the fair weather. The Dinato home was a safe haven for any child. Often when the boys were having a bonfire down at their pond their friends would wander up just to talk. Ellen and Daniel would listen intently and offer advice if asked but mostly they were just merely sounding boards. They were people who listened. That seemed to be the most important aspect of these visits. Ellen and Daniel would often marvel at the fact that these kids would rather be up in the house talking to two old fogies than down with the crew laughing and telling jokes. Sometimes these kids' parents were going through rough patches or in the throes of divorce. Some of the kids had no clue as to their future endeavors and would bounce ideas off of them. Whatever the reason, the Dinato's were "adoptive parents" to several boys and girls and were very proud of it. Ironically Ellen told Jeff that when Daniel and she married, they wanted to have a dozen children. After

Sonny was born they realized what a responsibility and financial commitment one child was so they down-sized to six. But as fate would have it, they could only have three. Ellen had always secretly yearned for at least one more baby. But as the children grew and the Dinato household became the magnet house for children, they realized that they did indeed have at least a dozen children at one point in time or another. Even though it was intrusive at times, Ellen and Daniel were quite happy to share their family and open their door to others. Jeff mulled over the many facts he had learned about this family and about Ellen. He grew more intrigued by the day by this woman. She was special.

CHAPTER 8

SUNDAY MORNING ALWAYS found them having a big breakfast and then going off to mass. This Sunday was no exception. Three days had gone by and there was no contact from the stalker. Ellen was hoping that no news was good news. She could only wish that the stalker had grown weary of trying to frighten her and had crawled back to his hole. Daniel was home for the weekend and was hurrying everybody along to church. The morning was quite cold and they were looking forward to coming home, having a fire and enjoying some homemade pasta and sauce.

At mass the congregation was all a buzz about the trivial daily comings and goings. The Dinato family was greeted as usual and they spoke to friends and neighbors. The homily today was about forgiveness. The priest was telling the congregation that forgiveness is such a gift. He explained that holding on to a grudge or a hurt only hurts the person holding on. It is counterproductive and drags on a situation that could be healed in moments just by forgiving your trespasser. Ellen thought to her self that they had had a trespasser recently on more than one occasion and that that was a tough task. After going to the parish center for coffee and goodies, Ellen, Daniel and Frankie went to get into their car. They weren't far when Frankie noticed the tires. All four had been slashed and were flatter than the pancakes they had had that morning. Daniel was instantly incensed and he swore right in the church parking lot. Ellen looked around to see how many people heard him. She was embarrassed but quietly livid. "This has got to stop", yelled Daniel. Ellen looked mystified as to what she could do to make it stop. Their Sunday had just been ruined by this person who apparently wasn't going to quit. Their neighbors waited with them until the tow truck driver got there and helped load the car on the carrier to be fixed the next day. The neighbors, Kelly and Keith, took them home and tried to keep the conversation light but Daniel was not in any mood to be sociable. He didn't say a word until he got home and then thanked them and said good-bye. Keith tried to make a funny and told Daniel to remember the topic of the homily – forgiveness. But it fell on deaf ears. Daniel stomped toward the house. He turned and just glowered and Ellen said her good-byes and her apologies. She knew that Daniel was feeling very frustrated and helpless to affect a change in the situation. At this point they didn't know who, what, or why this was happening and they were just like puppets on a string at the whim of this stalker.

After they all changed their clothes they busied themselves with odd jobs. Ellen worked on making her meatballs and sausage, Frankie was working on a report on the computer upstairs, and Daniel was laying a fire. This fireplace had a great draw and when they built the house they were amazed that so much of the heat actually stayed in the house. As Daniel knelt to light the craftily stacked array, the room started to fill with smoke. "Now what?", yelled Daniel. It only took a few seconds and the family room started to cloud up with smoke. Daniel opened and closed the flue several times and it was not jammed. But the smoke kept pouring in. He instantly ran to the sun room and threw open the doors. He screamed for Frankie to get down stairs and move the cars out of the garage and then the fire alarm built into their alarm system started to screech. It wasn't the kind that you could disconnect when it bothered you so it continued to make a hideous loud shriek. Ellen was running around trying to figure out what to do. Daniel grabbed the metal wood carrier and started placing the burning wood on the metal then he yelled at Ellen to dump the wood on the brick patio. She made several trips to dump the wood but the house was still swarming in a dense grey cloud of smoke. The next thing they knew the first volunteer fireman roared up the driveway in his pickup. He arrived before the trucks and his fellow volunteers because he lived only a mile up the road. Daniel told him what happened and after they opened several other windows and started the ceiling fan in the kitchen, the volunteer started to investigate. He shone a flashlight up the flue and couldn't see any sky. This was odd because the Dinato's not only got their chimney swept each fall, but they also had a cap on the top of the chimney so that animals couldn't get down in and nest. Sure enough, Daniel peered up and couldn't see any light. In the next few minutes the fire team arrived and the hunt was on. They stretched a ladder up to the steep roof and one of them bravely climbed up to peer into the chimney. "Here's the culprit", he said and pulled out a sooty old woolen Army blanket. They all stared in disbelief. And then it dawned on the Dinato's what was going on. "It's him again", said Ellen. "But how in the world did he get up there?" "There are tracks in the snow and marks similar to what our ladder is creating right next to the chimney wall. The foot prints are pretty big. "Probably wearing a boot", said the volunteer. Daniel was so angry he didn't know what to do. What a day. "What next?" he thought.

After all the commotion was over and the neighbors wandered off from their curiosity seeking, Daniel called Jeff. "This has got to stop"! yelled Daniel. Jeff knew that Daniel was at his breaking point. "Could you please come out and see if we can't come up with a plan to stop all this?" he asked. Jeff reassured him that he would be right out. This time he picked up agent Malone and they both came out. On the way out he reiterated all of their trials and tribulations on this Sunday. The tires could be replaced at a cost and his home wasn't permanently damaged thanks to their quick thinking. But, what's next?

As they pulled in the drive they saw that the cars were still out in the drive.... At least Frankie's and Ellen's. They asked Frankie to pull the cars in and shut the door. They found Daniel and Ellen sitting in the family room staring at each other. He didn't know what words had passed but he knew that there was tension in the air. In fact Ellen had been apologizing to Daniel and Frankie for getting them in this mess. Daniel was still fuming from the day's mishaps and was a mix of frustration, relief that no one was hurt, and fatigue at having to literally put out fires.

After Frankie came back into the house Jeff called them all together. He said that they were going to do some brainstorming. He got out a legal pad and made a time line from the first incident with the crow to the latest chimney sabotage. They all shared bits of information about each event and then they started to talk about who they thought could possibly be at the bottom of this whole ordeal. The Dinato's told the agents that they did not know of any Nazi activity in their area. Nothing was ever said about anything like this in their town or school. That left either strangers or the Van Eyck's. Agent Malone had looked into the Van Eyck family and had just a meager explanation of their past. "They have kept their noses clean here but I do think it is odd that they never asked for citizenship in the US. It makes you wonder if they could stand up under the scrutiny and a real check into their past. If you don't make waves – you don't get noticed." He went on to further explain that the information Ellen had given them was to the letter what he was able to find out. They were supposedly born in Holland, immigrated to Argentina and then on to the US. They supposedly only had one living child. She had worked as a seamstress from the home and he as a janitor. No waves – no notice. He said that he did have some of his people looking into immigration records to see if they could find out anything further. They had questioned the neighbors surreptitiously and they found that the old couple kept to themselves and never bothered anybody. They were very quiet and very serious. Nothing stood out.

Daniel told the agents that he was taking off from work for the next couple of days and he was installing instant lights all around his house. It wouldn't necessarily help during the day but they would know if something happened at night. He didn't want any more surprises. Jeff said that that was a good idea. Daniel was also purchasing an alarm to tell them who drove up the drive. Since their driveway was two acres long, he was going to place it half way up. Then they would know that some one was serious about coming up this long lane.

Jeff also explained that most of the incidents, although unnerving and very irritating, were minor, with the exception of poisoning the dogs. But they were taking this very seriously. "We would rather err on the side of caution than pass this off as just a nuisance situation." the agents clarified. The whole family was relieved to hear that they were getting some help.

It was Ellen who asked the agents if they thought an old man could be capable of these sorts of things. They answered her that where there was a will there was a way. Then she asked if it would be a smart move for the press to get involved. So far Ellen had said nothing to the townspeople about what was happening. Her friends and neighbors knew that someone was trying to frighten her and that there were some things that had transpired but the general public didn't know. "What if I write a story directed to this stalker?", she asked. "I don't think it is a good idea", said Jeff, but agent Malone responded that maybe that was an idea to flush this person out. "It would also make the general public aware to be on the look out for a man in a dark blue late model car with tinted windows. You know how much the Amber Alert helps out. What do we have to lose?", he queried. Their lives, thought Jeff.

They were agreed that Ellen would contact the Albany and Schenectady papers and work with one of their writers. The agents gave their permission to be mentioned as to looking into these strange circumstances. At least they were working on something and not just spinning their wheels in frustration – what was left of them.

As Ellen readied for bed that night she was mulling over what had transpired in one short day. She laughed to herself at the priest's homily on forgiveness and thought that the priest might think differently if these things were happening to him. But then she realized that the priest was a priest and he would try his best to practice what he preached. Ellen was going to have a tougher time than that.

CHAPTER 9

MONDAY DAWNED WITH a crisp Adirondack morning. The air was fresh, the sky was pure blue, and the breeze that whisked through the empty trees whistled their familiar song. After Daniel left to take Frankie to school, Ellen contacted the newspapers. Both papers were willing to cooperate and they took notes on the story which Ellen had written. The story was going to appear the next morning and they promised to give it a prominent spot. News of a local celebrity was very welcome and quite readable. The locals felt a kinship to events that were happening to one of their own.

As Ellen was readying for another day, Jeff called. She told him about the newspapers' willingness to cooperate and he was pleased. He told her that he was having the field office in Rochester, where Willem Van Eyck was living, look much more seriously into his whereabouts and hopefully more into his past. Ellen said that she thought that it was a long shot because he had to be in his late seventies or early eighties and he lived so far away. She didn't think that it was feasible for Van Eyck to travel back and forth so many times in the beginning of winter and accomplish the vandalism and attempts on their lives as the stalker had. He told her that he would report back to them that evening and let them know what they had learned. Ellen knew he was a bachelor so she automatically invited him to dinner. Often times she would ask men out to the house for dinner when Daniel was home and who Daniel worked with who were working in the local office and away from home. She knew what a treat it was for these men to eat a home cooked meal with a family instead of by themselves in a restaurant. A few years of that kind of solitude and fare got really tiring. Jeff was no exception. He automatically accepted.

That evening, Jeff arrived and smelled something heavenly. Ellen told him that she was fixing one of Daniel's favorite dinners that wasn't Italian. In fact it was from Ellen's heritage from the Midwest. So much of the cooking from the farm lands had an ethnic background. The early settlers brought their recipes with them and passed them on over the years. This one was a basted pork roast with peas, sauerkraut and roasted potatoes all topped with caraway seeds. He also smelled homemade bread. Ellen confessed that in recent years she had gotten lazier and purchased a bread machine to help her with the kneading. After several years, she had wearied of the time it took to properly prepare the dough for baking. Jeff told her that he was just pleased that he could have homemade bread. Daniel watched with interest as Jeff and Ellen talked so freely. It was if they had known each other for years. He was used to Ellen being the perfect hostess, but this time there was a tinge of intimacy that she had always saved just for Daniel. But he realized that these were extraordinary times and that she probably was very relieved to have a special guardian who was taking such interest in her situation. Never in the twenty four years of marriage had Daniel been jealous; never had he ever doubted her fidelity. And he reminded himself that he was being foolish now and should knock it off.

Jeff went on and on about the dinner and Daniel was glad that it was over and they could get down to some serious conversation. Daniel explained that he had installed the lights and the driveway alarm during the day and he was satisfied that they were more protected. He explained that he was going to stay home tomorrow and just make sure everything was battened down and then he had to leave on Wednesday for negotiations in Florida. Both Ellen and Jeff looked at him covetously to be able to bask in the warm sun away from the long, cold winter that was just starting in upper state New York. But Ellen knew that Daniel never got a chance to just sit in the sun and read a book. The best he could do was to get in a round of golf but most of the time he spent in the inside of cabs, conferences rooms, hotel rooms and airplanes. She knew it wasn't all that glamorous but she still envied him the freedom to jet back and forth to so many places.

As they settled down in the family room with their coffee, and Frankie disappeared upstairs, Jeff told him that the Rochester field agents had queried the neighbors of Van Eyck's further and that they got the same picture as before. They also realized that once again he was not in his bungalow. In fact the neighbors thought it was unusual for this time of year. It was common practice for Van Eyck to park his car in his attached one car garage and the only way that the neighbors knew he was home was the dull glow of light that peeked through the heavy curtains on all the windows. He was reported to get up early and go to bed early because of his hours of working as a janitor. He never had caused a moment's trouble and he just kept to himself and didn't bother anyone. The only time he was seen was when he pulled in or out of his driveway and garage or took the trash out. He was like clockwork. He left at 6:20 and came home at 4:20. Rarely was he seen outside and the only time the neighborhood children saw him was on Halloween when he silently passed out candy to the gaily costumed ghosts and goblins. At Christmas he put a wreath on his door but they never knew whether he had a Christmas tree or not because his curtains were always closed. They didn't know how Mrs. Van Eyck, when she was alive, had had clients for her sewing because no one ever came to the house. They reported that in the summer he always had had a neighbor boy mow the lawn and in the winter shovel his walk and driveway which was kind of a frill for the other neighbors who tended to their homes themselves. The brick bungalow was situated in a blue collar neighborhood with very small lawns and not much room between houses. Row after row of two and three bedroom homes stood like little soldiers at ready. There wasn't much to differentiate the homes but some people had gotten more creative and changed the color of their shutters or added a little patch of picket fencing. But they were all pretty much the same.

The neighbors to Van Eyck's north seemed to be more knowledgeable about the Van Eyck's than any one else. It seemed that they had lived in the neighborhood since shortly after their marriage and the husband was ready to retire in a couple of years. The wife had always stayed at home and been a housewife and she had a lot of spare time on her hands; time that she tried to share with her neighbors but the Van Eyck's were the one exception to any socializing. The neighbors to the north had watched other people move in and out of their neighborhood, but they were the neighbors who had the longevity. Again they reported that the Van Eyck's had always stayed to themselves and never socialized with any one. The only thing that was unusual was that they seemed to travel a lot. It was not uncommon for them to be gone three out of every four weekends of the month. After their daughter married and moved away, they still continued to be gone at those times. Each summer they would take a three week vacation. The neighbors had no clue where they went and the only way they knew they were gone was because they didn't see them coming or going and then three weeks later his routine would start anew. Now that Mrs. Van Eyck was gone they only had him to watch. Small neighborhoods make great "neighborhood watch" locations because everyone was on top of everyone else and it was a bit obvious as to someone's comings and goings. And if there were any yelling or screaming the neighbors caught all of it – especially in the summer. But the neighbors never heard a peep out of the Van Eyck's.

Jeff also found out from the field agents' report that Mr. Van Eyck hadn't been seen recently. The irony was that with the amount of anti-social behavior from Van Eyck, he could be in his house dead as a doornail and the neighbors would never know. Their mail was never delivered so they must have had a post office box and they didn't subscribe to any paper. So the neighbors wondered aloud if he was OK. The field agents knocked at his door but no one answered and there was no sign of any one about. His trash can was beside his house and hadn't been filled. There were no lights that could be seen day or night and because the curtains were always drawn, the agents couldn't even peek in the house. None of the neighbors could remember ever being told where Mr. Van Eyck worked but they all knew he was a janitor. Or at least that is what they had been told. The house had no signs of anything extravagant. The garage housed only one car and was basically empty, and according to the neighbors there wasn't anything stored in the garage when they had seen him coming and going. The garage side door even had a heavy curtain on it and the garage door was a solid aging wood. So, there was no way of knowing if his car was in the garage or not. Van Eyck's car was registered as a 15 year old red Toyota and he was insured. The Van Eyck's had never used a credit card – even for gas and they had one checking account with $2,500.00 in it. The IRS had reported that Mr. Van Eyck had religiously reported his salary for tax purposes and was employed by the Millabro Company. He made approximately $37,000 a year and had taken out for all of the appropriate deductions. He had a thirty year mortgage and his payment was $389.00 a month. His purchase price had been minimal and he had never been late with a mortgage payment. He had a savings account with approximately $5,500.00 in it, not a lot to show for all of his years of work and simple living. The Millabro Company, reported to be a consulting firm with headquarters in Chicago, had an office building in Rochester and that is apparently where Mr. Van Eyck went to work every week day. When the agents stopped in to pay a visit to the Millabro Company, they found a receptionist who was all business and no personality. She informed him that Mr. Van Eyck had indeed been employed there for many years as their janitor and was an ideal employee. She also told them that Mr. Van Eyck was supposedly on vacation and didn't know where he was. They asked if they could speak to someone in charge and they were told that that gentleman was out of town on business and wouldn't be back for several days. The stark sterile environment of the diminutive office didn't seem at all welcoming and the agents left. The lack of forthcoming information was disturbing. They wondered why Mr. Van Eyck would possibly go to work in this place but ironically it fit in with the description of his anti-social behavior. Even though he was quite a lot older and able to retire, he usually reported to work anyway. This could be explained away by being a lonely widower with nothing else to do. And even though he was getting up in years, his neighbors said that he seemed very healthy and stood ram rod straight and moved like a much younger man.

Jeff also said, "I always have red lights going off when I hear of someone being so reclusive. It always makes me think that someone has something that they want to hide". Daniel and Ellen were told that the Rochester agents were going to look into the "disappearance" of Mr. Van Eyck and they were going to keep an eye on his house. The agents also decided to enter his home because the neighbors had wondered about his welfare and his lock proved to be easy to pop open. When they entered the small home it was very neat but with a musty old smell.

That was probably because of the heavy draperies which hung from the tops of the windows and the fact that the house apparently hadn't been opened up and aired out for a very long time. The draperies looked very dusty. There were a few family pictures, mostly of vacation times, but no Mr. Van Eyck. As they searched through the rest of the house they found that the two bedrooms were unoccupied and that everything was quite well kept. Nothing was expensive in the house. Even the kitchen didn't have a lot of modern conveniences. There was an empty coffee machine and a toaster and that was it. The refrigerator had a minimum amount of food and a couple of bottles of wine. There were glass beer bottles on the lower shelf and some cheese and sandwich makings. There really was not much that would spoil in a few days and there was no milk, which they found odd. They checked the trash and they found it empty – also odd. This meant that Mr. Van Eyck's leaving was most likely planned. They looked around until they found where Mr. Van Eyck kept his personal papers. There was an old desk in his bedroom, or what they assumed was his bedroom. The other bedroom had nothing in the closet or the dresser. The desk held the usual utility bills and expense receipts but nothing out of the ordinary. For all intents and purposes they were just looking at a bungalow belonging to an older man who had very little. There were no surprises and learned nothing new. In fact it was surprisingly devoid of much personal. For a person who had lived as long as he did, Mr. Van Eyck didn't seem to be very sentimental. There was a picture of Mrs. Van Eyck which looked like it had been taken maybe tens years before her death and a few pictures of their daughter. One was from her high school graduation and one from her wedding.

Ellen had been at that wedding because she had to be and did not enjoy it in the least. Ellen did not enjoy any of their company and dreaded being in their presence even for half a day. In fact she was rather horrified to see the bizarre behavior of her sister-in-law's parents. But it once again reassured her that there was something not quite right about them. Ellen's presence was requested because Daniel stood up for his brother at the wedding. Being best man required that his wife be there or there would be hard feelings for years to come. So she swallowed her pride and went even though she knew it was going to be something for great story telling later. It lived up to this and then some.

The mother of the bride who for months was to be making all of the wedding dresses including the bridal gown was very secretive. She was even supposed to be making the groom's mother's dress. Daniel's mother started to feel uneasy about a month before the wedding and wondered why she hadn't been asked to come over for a fitting. The elder Mrs. Dinato was quite pleased at the idea of the mother making all of the gowns. But when she asked the future bride how the sewing was coming, the future daughter-in-law just rolled her eyes and said that the progress was slow. At two weeks before the wedding, Mrs. Dinato was actually thinking of going out and purchasing a dress just in case. Two days before the wedding the dress that she was assured would be ready was nowhere in sight. And the day before the wedding found all of the bridesmaids, the flower girl and Mrs. Dinato scrambling for something to wear. The bridesmaids asked friends if any of them had a pastel looking prom dress. All four of them ended up in dresses that didn't match and Mrs. Dinato ended up wearing a strapless evening gown that she had worn for a company party with her husband. For a Catholic wedding this was blasphemy and she felt totally sheepish doing it but it was all she had and there was not enough time to go out and find one and have it altered to her short height. Mrs. Dinato, Daniel's mother, thought this was all very peculiar because this strange woman was supposed to be a professional seamstress. The only dress which was over half way finished was the bridal gown. She had nearly finished it but there was no zipper in the back. So the new sister-in-law was pinned into her dress which worked until about half way through the mass and some of the pins came loose when she went up to light the candle for the blessed Virgin Mary, and her dress was gaping open in the back. The congregation got a shock as she stood there with her back to them and was half way dressed.

This was not the only snafu. The mother of the bride put a real wrench in the works when she refused to go to the wedding. The congregation waited in the church in the sweltering July humidity for over two hours. The priest was incensed but was at least relieved that he didn't have another wedding that afternoon. After waiting two hours, the bride finally drove back to her house and picked her mother up. The bride- to- be had been putting on a scene of histrionics about every ten minutes because her mother was refusing to appear. But when they returned to the church, the bride's mother refused to walk down the aisle when the mothers were seated and secretly sneaked in when Mrs. Dinato was being seated and the congregation's heads were turned. And Ellen thought it was most odd that Mrs. Van Eyck refused to have her picture taken for any of the wedding photos.

The reception was quite meager and the atmosphere loaded with tension. The Van Eyck's put in an appearance and then left. The Dinato's and their friends and relatives thought all of this was quite odd but then the Van Eyck's weren't Italian and they thought that maybe their traditions were very different and their budget very small. Italians put on such a spread and it is always such a time of merriment and celebration that the receptions are usually quite noisy and memorable. This reception was memorable all right but for far different reasons.

The unfortunate outcome of this strange union was that Daniel's brother and the weird sister-in-law had separated themselves from the rest of the family. They lived several hundred miles away and now had almost nothing to do with the family. This was a tragedy in an Italian family. Italians families are bonded with each other. They may yell and fight over nothing but when push comes to shove they are there for each other and for every celebration. Daniel's brother had forgotten this trait and they were all saddened when he was mentioned.

As Jeff finished telling Daniel and Ellen about what was discovered, he told them that they were going to try to see if they couldn't find out more about his whereabouts. They were going to use his New York State driver's license photo and run a blurb in the Rochester paper and a quick blurb for the local TV stations about a missing person (a person of interest) and see if any one knew of his whereabouts. They were going to ask him to come in for questioning and that is all that they said.

They were going to hold off on the Albany and Schenectady papers for another day or two. But their aim was to see if anyone out there knew any more about this elusive man.

Jeff called it a night and told them that he would be in touch tomorrow and they might know more about Mr. Van Eyck or whatever his name was. Daniel and Ellen thanked him for coming over and for showing such concern for their problem. He told them that it was his pleasure and that this was just part of his job. Ellen and Daniel both knew that this was actually above and beyond what they thought a normal agent would do. They didn't know quite why but Mr. Portman had an affinity for the Dinato's. Daniel had his suspicions and Ellen's weren't too far off the mark. She was flattered and was complimented that at her age she could impress someone and be a cause for so much attention. She was so used to being taken for granted; she had actually not thought about being the center of attention in a romantic way for a very long time. Motherhood and all of her other duties took the forefront and romance and appeal were way back in the cobwebs of time.

Jeff represented the urgent feelings of interest and excitement. He was virile and attractive and definitely interested in Ellen. She could feel it. Theirs was a magnetic attraction. He stirred feelings in her that she thought had been killed off years ago. She took great pains now in preparing her special meals. She took more time in her appearance and she was interested in life once again. Between the writing and now the fantasizing, Ellen was coming back to life. "So why don't I feel totally happy about it?" she wondered. "Because you're married, dummy, married and in a committed relationship. And you have children who would be terribly marred if you had an indiscretion, not to mention Daniel," "You will just have to suck up those new feelings and carry on. It certainly is nice to think about, but to act on this would not only be immoral but it would affect so many people that it is not worth the damage and upheaval, but I can still picture this in my mind, can't I? There is no harm in that!"

Ellen often mused over time, that after the children arrived, a couple's romantic relationship usually atrophied. Left in its wake was a friendship – or they couldn't stand to be with each other. This friendship was an echo of the past feelings and bond. Ellen truly loved Daniel and would for life. But she was discouraged that the amorous aspect of their relationship had slipped to last place. Daniel had his business concerns which definitely took the gold medal; then came the children and lastly, Ellen. Ellen also intellectually knew that Daniel on some level truly loved her. But she didn't usually feel it. She felt misplaced and taken for granted. Divorce was not in Daniel's vocabulary. He would rather die than divorce. But Ellen sometimes wondered if it was the blasphemous breaking of the religious rite or if he would never want to leave her – no matter what.

As usual Ellen listened to the familiar rhythm of Daniel getting ready for bed. He did the same things in the same order every night. She could tell <u>him </u>what was next. As she settled in her bed and picked up her latest read, she fantasized about having some other man in her life. She and Daniel had been married for so long and had such a history that she always thought that they would grow old together and die in each others arms. It had never occurred to her that it wouldn't be with Daniel. When he flew so much, she used to worry about the "what ifs". She wondered where she would go, if she would have to get a job, and how it would be to raise the boys alone. But now the boys were older and soon would be totally off on their own. The time for being together and having a second life was soon to be. But Daniel was so into his work that Ellen longed for someone to talk to and to romance her. Gone were the romantic evenings when they were foot loose and fancy free and quite amorous. All that was left were cloudy memories of a time when they were really a couple. Now they were more like roommates and it was sad. It was especially sad because now they had more financial freedom and someday time to do things. Soon the boys wouldn't even be in the house. This was a time when most people kicked up their heels and let loose but so far Daniel hadn't even noticed. It seemed that the older he got, the more he tried to achieve. His ambition for work hadn't diminished, if anything it was in super drive. But his drive to be a couple and connect with his wife was in the past – a mere memory. Apparently, he was quite comfortable with the arrangement the way it was. It was Ellen who seemed to be the one who was hurting. Especially after nurturing children as strongly as Ellen had, she had a void in her life for that caring. She even had asked Daniel about legally adopting a small child or becoming a foster parent but Daniel was not at all in favor of it. She had to live with that void and try to cope with her feelings. But it didn't make her happy and all of a sudden there was a bright spot in her life. A new man who loved her cooking, loved her talents, and could make her laugh like she used to. He complimented her and made a fuss about her. She was more than flattered, she downright enjoyed it. And her thoughts had been flitting to Jeff more than she would like them to. After all she was a married woman and this was just not right. But she could fanaticize, couldn't she?

The article about Van Eyck appeared in the Rochester paper and on the air. There were several tips phoned in to the Rochester field office. There were calls from his grocery store clerk from his neighborhood, the gas station he frequented, and an unusual call from a man from the other side of Rochester from where Mr. Van Eyck was living. He rented houses out in a poorer section of Rochester and he also had several garages that were not being used. So he rented those out for boat storage and other things. He said that a man had been renting a stall in one of his garages for several years. But that his name was not Mr. Van Eyck but was a Mr. Pieter Vermeer and he now stored a dark blue late model car in it. He had always paid on time and never caused any problems but he was surprised that this man in the paper looked so much like his renter. Not only did the agents' ears perk up about this but so did Jeff's. He thought that this would be one way to hide a nicer, newer car from the neighbors. But the obvious question was why.

Jeff called Tuesday and told Daniel and Ellen about their new findings. He was especially interested in the fact that Van Eyck had gone to the trouble of hiding a nice car from his neighbors. And the fact that he had used a different name was intriguing. The Dinato's agreed and were even more puzzled by this man. Jeff also told them that because of the Rochester findings that they were going to ask the local papers to run the article, too. Daniel and Ellen spent the day together checking all the windows and doors, making sure that the house was secure and trying to enjoy the peace and quiet free from any interruptions or any unnecessary excitement. They passed the day without incident.

Wednesday found Frankie off to school and Daniel off to the office. He was determined to try to stay close to home for the next week or two and had made alternative arrangements at work. He was thankful that they were understanding. As Ellen was cleaning the bathrooms she once again thought about the odd twist her life was taking. And it all came about because of her book, or more correctly, books. She marveled at the idea that so much excitement could happen in such a short period of time even though it was bizarre. Once again she let her mind drift to the subject of Jeff. Jeff was at least a couple of years younger than Ellen and she was feeling guilty but giddy even thinking of him. He was very physically fit and taller than Daniel. Daniel had pretty much kept his shape since their wedding, an accomplishment which always amazed Ellen because she hadn't. Childbirth had rearranged her shape and the extra pounds she carried were getting harder and harder to get rid of. Ellen didn't sincerely mind having a more Reubenesque figure because she knew that bearing her boys was definitely worth it. She knew deep in her heart that she was never meant to be a svelte model shape. But she secretly wished she could at least have the figure she had when she got married. But it didn't seem to bother Daniel and now she realized that apparently it didn't bother Jeff, either. So being a woman wasn't the same as being a girl and this was definitely one way that it differed. A day and a half had gone by without incident. Maybe the articles in the papers and the spots on the TV were enough to let Van Eyck or whatever his true name was know that he was now under scrutiny.

At noon, Ellen went into the kitchen to start to fix her lunch. As she was at the sink she noticed that the lights on their barn went on. These were the lights that were set off by a motion detector. She leaned farther over into the sink to try to get a better look out the window but she saw nothing. It could have been a cat or some other animal that set it off. She knew that if the dogs had been home they would have been raising a ruckus and no cat was stupid enough to trespass in the dogs' pen in the back yard. She kept peering out the window but there was nothing there. Daniel and she had seriously talked about getting another dog or dogs to replace Duchess and Copper but they decided that they were too frightened to risk the lives of any other animals with a crazy person out there. So they would have to go without their automatic doorbells from any dogs.

After Ellen had finished her lunch, she went into the laundry room to change loads. She heard a funny noise and waited with her heart in her throat. Nothing happened. And there was no other noise. She calmed herself and reassured herself that the alarm was on and she was perfectly fine. Just in case, she went to the front door and looked at the monitor for the alarm. It was set and on. She went back to the laundry room and tried to talk herself out of calling Daniel at the office. He would probably get upset with her for the inconvenience and probably tell her that it was all in her head. He wouldn't come home just for her nervousness and he would be miffed at the interruption. So she decided she would wait and call if something else happened.

As she was finishing putting the next load of dirty clothes in the washer she heard something else. It was like a far away bump. She went from one window to another and she didn't see a thing. There were windows on three sides of the house, but the North wall contained the fireplace wall and there were no windows. She decided that the noises were probably from the cold and the house was cracking because of the low temperature. As she ascended the stairs, Ellen was totally freaked out because the alarm went off. She dropped the clean clothes basket on the stairs and did the unthinkable. She went down stairs to look. When the alarm would go off there was a terrible shrieking siren that throbbed rhythmically. She had heard it on several occasions through the years when she forgot and walked in the house from the garage and forgot to disarm it. But this time she knew it wasn't a false alarm. She instinctively knew that something wasn't right. She felt sick at her stomach and her heart was up in her throat. As she rounded the corner from the hall into the kitchen she knew why. There in the doorway to the kitchen stood the very tall frame of Mr., Van Eyck – or whatever his real name was. He was sneering and looked quite pleased with himself. Ellen could hardly speak. Between the blaring siren and her frightened state, she could barely get out, "What are you doing here? Don't you know that the police are going to be here in just a few minutes?" Then she stopped and thought how lame that was. She wished that the police car would be screaming down her driveway this very minute. But she knew from past experience on false alarms that the local authorities would be at least fifteen minutes in responding. Van Eyck just kept sneering at her. He said in his heavily accented English, "Oh no my dear, quite to the contrary. You see I have cut the phone lines. Your alarm will work in your house but it cannot signal the monitoring company that anything is wrong. You know the alarm is going off, but they don't. In fact if it would help, you can turn it off now because it will do you no further good. Ellen didn't move. So Van Eyck advanced toward her. She backed up until she hit the wall. She started to turn toward the front door and thought of trying to make a run for it but the door was not only dead bolted, but it was locked as well. She would never make it. She punched in her code and the screeching stopped. Slowly Ellen turned around to face him to see what was going to happen next and she saw his big hand go up to her face. She smelled a weird smell on his handkerchief and then everything went black.

The next thing she knew was that she was in someplace dark. She woke up groggily and couldn't recognize a thing and then she came to the realization that she was moving. She was in someplace dark and moving. Her brain whirled trying to make sense of her situation. She then remembered the sneering face of Van Eyck and she had the sinking, sickening feeling that this was probably it. In fact, Ellen couldn't figure out why he hadn't killed her right there in her own home if he wanted to get rid of her. None of this made any sense. She came to the realization quickly that she wasn't wearing a coat and it was freezing. She also realized that she was in a trunk but she couldn't move. She tried to move her hands and they were tied behind her back. She tried to move her legs which were cramping but they were tied also and were connected to the ties to her hands. She felt like a calf at a rodeo. There was duct tape over her mouth so she couldn't scream. All of the tricks she had learned and read about over the years about getting away from a kidnapper couldn't be used now. She couldn't knock out the tail lights, or fiddle with the trunk lid, or even make much noise. Her heart sank when she realized her predicament. She didn't know how long she had been unconscious but the car was still moving. She was suddenly hit with the idea that she probably wouldn't ever see Daniel or the boys again. Tears streamed down her face and she silently cursed herself for even starting to write her books. Why couldn't she have chosen some safe hobby like painting or something? But here she was and she desperately tried to think of a way out of this mess. The harder she thought the more hopeless it seemed. And besides, she was shaking so much from the cold that she thought she might just die right there in the trunk. And then the car stopped.

When Frankie got home from school, he entered his quiet home. Ellen usually had the TV on at this time of day and was watching some talk show or interior design program. But there was just silence. And then he remembered that he should have seen the red light on the alarm pad. But he had just walked right in like he used to and he totally had forgotten about the alarm. He walked back out and stared at the alarm pad. It was green and nothing had been set. Then he walked back in and called for his mom. Silence. Then he got scared. "Mom", he yelled. And he started to run through the house. He was screaming for her but there was no answer. He searched every room and even the basement. He went back into the garage and saw her car sitting there and he really got frightened. He walked around the house and saw fresh foot prints beside the side of the house. He ran back into the house and reached for the phone in the kitchen to call for help and too call his Dad. There was no note on the counter and his mom always told the boys where she was going. All of a sudden it dawned on him that there was no dial tone. He had been sitting there waiting to make a call and it then occurred to him that there was no noise in his phone. He still had his coat on and he dashed out the door and ran to their neighbor's house. Fortunately they were home and he called the authorities immediately. Then he called his dad. That was the worst. Daniel was totally frightened and harried. He told Frankie that he would be home as soon as he could get there. He also told him to stay at the neighbors and he would pick him up. Daniel must have broken all the speed limits getting home but he was there just after the police got there. On his way home Daniel also called Jeff and told him what happened. Jeff was shocked but immediately rebounded and told Daniel that he would be there as fast as he could.

After Daniel picked up a very shaken Frankie, he roared up his driveway and saw two police cars. The first belonged to the town constable and the next belonged to the county sheriff's department. The two men were waiting outside of their cars and conferring. Apparently the constable was filling the sheriff's deputy about what had been transpiring as of the last few days. The deputy told the constable that they had heard most of it and were aware that there were some hinky things going on out here. Daniel greeted both men and introduced them to his son. Daniel dreaded going into the house but he wanted to know what was going on. As they entered the garage, Daniel looked at the alarm panel. Everything looked in order. Then they went into the kitchen. Nothing looked out of order. And then he went over and tried the phone. It was dead all right. He looked quizzically at the officers and they then asked him where the phone lines came into the house. Daniel informed them that the power lines were buried and therefore the alarm could be disarmed that way. The officers informed Daniel that as long as the electricity was going to the alarm pads that everything would work fine in the house. But if someone were smart enough to snip the telephone wires, the alarm message would not reach alarm headquarters. Daniel walked the officers out to the back side of the house nearest the barn and then they saw why. The lines to the telephone had definitely been snipped and they had no phone service to the whole house. They all knew what this meant. Ellen was gone.

Just then they heard another car roaring up the driveway. Daniel walked around the side of the house and saw Jeff speeding toward the garage. Jeff looked as distressed as Daniel. Slowly Daniel started telling Jeff what he had found or more truthfully, not found. Jeff inspected the cut lines and went through the house with Daniel and Frankie. This got to be too much for Frankie and tears started forming in his eyes. Not wanting to make a scene Frankie excused himself and went up to his room and shut the door. Daniel was rather relieved that he had because now he could speak more frankly with the officers and Jeff. They sat down at the kitchen table and discussed what would be happening in the next few hours. Jeff told Daniel that initially that the local authorities would be running the show. They had discussed this and it made sense for the locals to be the front men and Jeff would provide extra help. Since they didn't know if she had been transported over state lines the FBI didn't have much jurisdiction. The two officers genuinely nodded and they went on to explain to Daniel about what they needed from him and how they were to conduct themselves in the next few hours. Daniel and Frankie were requested to stay home and to stay near the phone which was being fixed. They were going to put a tap on the phone but they had their doubts as to whether they would be contacted or not. It seemed it was only Ellen that the stalker was interested in and the subject of her next book. The local officers were secretly not optimistic about her return and said that they were obviously dealing with a disturbed individual. Daniel knew this already having dealt with all of the stalker's dirty tricks and the loss of his two pets. Daniel was also running the worst case scenario through his mind and he didn't even want to think that. But he knew that she hadn't left of her own free will. Her purse and her coat were still in the hall closet. Daniel knew that this did not look good – not good at all.

CHAPTER 10

WHEN THE CAR stopped Ellen wondered not only where she was but how long it had taken to get here. With a shiver she remembered that Van Eyck had stuffed something in her face on his handkerchief and then everything went black. Now she heard the car door open and footsteps coming toward her. The trunk was opened by a remote button and the lid flew open to expose Van Eyck looking at her with that strange sneer. He said in his accented English, "Well, well, well, look what we have here." And then he laughed a maniacal laugh. Ellen's eyes bulged out with fear and she realized that they were in a warm garage. She knew it would be a while before her shivering would stop but at least she was now in out of the cold.

"Welcome to my home", he laughed. He then proceeded to help Ellen get out of the trunk. He had to snip the rope which attached her hands to her feet and he cut the rope that had her feet tied together. She could not walk at all well because her feet had gone to sleep being so cramped up and immobile. But she felt the unusually strong hands of Van Eyck leading her into his home. Ellen knew that this was not the home in Rochester because this was a large three car garage. As she was walking, she noticed her new surroundings. Everything was anally tidy and everything was erect in its place. He helped her up a set of stairs and they entered into a very large kitchen. The kitchen was state of the art and had a great deal of industrial sized appliances. Her eyes swept to the light which was streaming through the front windows which overlooked a large lake. All of the other side windows in the living room were heavily draped and blanketed the light from coming in. She could tell by the size of the trees that this living room was up at least two to three stories. No wonder he didn't need curtains on the front window. He had complete privacy if he wanted it. Ellen was amazed at the elegance and the extravagance of this home. Could he possibly own this? The difference between his home in Rochester and this lake property was ludicrous, but then Ellen mused why should anything about this man surprise her?

He placed her in an expensive looking over-stuffed chair but kept her hands tied behind her back. He viciously ripped the duct tape off of her mouth and watched her face with satisfaction as tears welled up in her eyes. He was obviously enjoying her pain. "Why are you doing this?" she asked with a trembling voice. She still hadn't warmed up but she wasn't shaking nearly as much.

Van Eyck said, "In time, in time". He then cut the rope with a sharp knife which had been binding her hands and she shook them to get the circulation back. He placed the knife next to the chair on the end table. He said, "Don't get too comfortable now and he removed a roll of duct tape from his coat. He proceeded to wrap the tape around Ellen in the chair so she couldn't move and she was very frightened. "What do you want?" asked Ellen. Van Eyck just chuckled in an evil way. "As I said, in time, in time".

He then busied himself in the kitchen and was starting a pot of coffee. He was apparently hungry and he prepared lunch for himself and not for Ellen. He then sat on a bar stool at the bar island in the kitchen and ate his lunch. He seemed quite pleased with himself and he would insanely chuckle every now and then, over what ever he was thinking about in his head. This made Ellen cringe with every laugh. She now knew that Van Eyck or whoever he really was, was definitely at least one sandwich short of a picnic. She knew enough from her teaching experience and work with psychology that Van Eyck was extremely unbalanced but quite intelligent and cagey.

Back at the Dinato's, the officers had left to start the ball rolling. Jeff stayed on for a little while trying to ease Daniel and Frankie's concern. Before he left, he called Rochester's field office and requested that the agents once again go into Van Eyck's home and search for any clues as to where he might have taken Ellen. There were just too many threads of this case that lead straight to Van Eyck and they all were not focused on anyone else. The agents said they would get right on it. Shortly after Jeff walked back into his office he got a call from the Rochester agents. They were in Van Eyck's Rochester residence and had gone through searching for anything. There was no paper trail for him owning any other residence or renting any other property. They had called the man who rented Van Eyck his garage and he had gone over to check to see if his car was there and he had reported back that it was gone. That fit.

The agents had a hand held photographic cell phone and they were sending images of the contents of Van Eyck's home to Jeff. They said, "Do you remember how odd we said it was that there was only one picture of Mrs. Van Eyck in the whole home? Well, we looked closely at the photo and she is standing next to a beautiful lake home with a lot of private land. Initially it looks like they were vacationing at a lodge but now that we know he owns an expensive new car, possibly he has another life with another much nicer home." Jeff considered this and thought it was definitely a lead to follow up on. He thanked them for their time and told them to continue looking and call if they found anything new.

Jeff walked into Agent Malone's office and told him about the phone call. Michael Malone agreed wholeheartedly and said that he would begin searching the database for real estate holdings at all of the lakes in New York. If Van Eyck had been using his second home for a home base through the last few weeks, it probably wasn't more than two or three hours away. But he said he would check everywhere. Jeff reminded him to not only check under Van Eyck but also to include Pieter Vermeer in his search.

The locals had all ready put out an APB on the late model navy blue Mercedes. In this neck of the woods, it was more common to see pick up trucks and four wheel drive vehicles than it was to see luxury cars. In the summer the tourists from "the city" and New Jersey came up in every description of vehicle but in the rough winter weather, the locals were much more practical. They had to be.

Jeff tried to busy himself but he had a personal connection to this kidnapping and his mind kept reeling about Ellen. After his second cup of coffee, Malone appeared at his office door and cried, "Bingo!" A Dr. Pieter Vermeer owns a large lake home at Bern Lake just north of here. It is probably no more than an hour and a half drive. Jeff was mobilized. He immediately jumped up from his desk and said, "Let's go!" Agent Malone stopped him and said just a minute. We need to coordinate with the local authorities in that county and have them waiting for us nearby when we get up there. Jeff hurriedly said, "We can do that on the way up. Let's go". Michael Malone had only been with Agent Portman for a year. Jeff had attended his wedding and they had socialized some and he knew him well enough that this haste was out of character for him. He was usually a plodding analytical thinker and doer. Now he was letting his heart lead the way instead of his head. He knew that Jeff was emotionally bonded to Ellen from watching him talk about her. He had spent an inordinate amount of time describing his visits to him. Her hospitality, her good cooking, her sense of humor even through this whole ordeal, these were all things he raved about. This was totally uncharacteristic of him. Michael knew he was smitten but he didn't know the depth of his emotions until now.

Jeff and Michael left instructions with another agent to check into the neighbors of his Lake Bern home and see if they knew anything. And then they speedily left. Michael decided he would drive because he could see how shaken Jeff was. Jeff thought it was a good idea to call Daniel and tell them that they had a lead. When Daniel answered he sounded totally stressed. Jeff explained the new information which they had just received and told him that they were on their way up to Lake Bern and to see if that is where Van Eyck/Vermeer had Ellen. Daniel wanted to go along and told them that he would meet them up at the Thruway exit right before Lake Bern, but Jeff knew better than to take an emotional family member along. He told Daniel that he would be of much better use by standing by the phone for any other news. Daniel begrudgingly agreed and they hung up.

About half way up to Lake Bern, Jeff's cell phone rang. "Agent Portman", he answered. It was the agent out of his home office who he had asked to check on Lake Bern and the neighbors. "Very interesting", said Jeff. Then the agent proceeded to tell Jeff what he had learned. "It seems that our Dr. Vermeer does indeed have a lake home and he has followed the same aloof behavior which he exhibited in Rochester. The Vermeer's bought a five acre tract fifteen years ago and had this lovely home built on a private section of the land. We talked with only two neighbors because several of the neighbors use their homes either just in the summer and fall or they were not at home. But the two we talked to were full of information. It seems that our Dr. Vermeer and his late wife were extremely anti-social. The Penn family, who live to their south, are very friendly, social people and up on all the comings and goings at Lake Bern. They had built two years before the Vermeer's and were happy to get new neighbors at the lake. Both Mr. and Mrs. Penn went over to welcome them to the neighborhood. Dr.Vermeer answered the door and the late Mrs. Vermeer seemed to shyly hide behind him. Mrs. Penn went through her spiel about welcoming them but Dr. Vermeer had just grunted a response. Mrs. Penn then went on to invite them over for a drink that evening and Dr. Vermeer told them that they didn't drink but thanked them and shut the door. The Penn's were quite taken aback by the brashness and rudeness of the Vermeer's and went home with lots to report to the other neighbors. The next morning when Mrs. Penn was driving past the Vermeer's she was shocked to see a couple of wine bottles sticking out of the top of their trash. She would continue to see this over the years and would laugh to herself every time she saw them. That first experience had set the pace for all other dealings with the Vermeer's. Initially the Penn's would wave to the Vermeer's when they would drive by, but after a few times it was obvious that the Vermeer's had absolutely no intention of being friendly so they just peacefully co-existed as neighbors. Mrs. Penn did say that they had walked through the Vermeer's house as it was being built and she knew what it was like inside but she had never again been inside to see what it looked like now. She also added that she had rarely seen any visitors come and go. Since the Vermeer's lot was so private, the only time they saw the doctor and his wife was when the Vermeer's were either swimming or lounging on their mammoth dock. They never spoke and they never paid any attention to any one else. The neighbor two houses to the north had the same type of experience. Although they had never gone over to visit, they had tried to wave and speak, but were met with a consistent cold shoulder, Even though the neighbors' houses were also expensive, lovely homes, somehow, the Vermeer's gave the impression that they were above the neighbors and didn't want to stoop to socialize with peons. At least that was the consensus of opinion in their area.

By now Ellen was starving between all of the adrenaline and nervous energy that she had expended, and the dusk hour, her stomach was rumbling and she was thirsty. She asked Van Eyck/Vermeer for a drink of water. He scoffed at her and told her that was not going to be necessary. Ellen wondered if she was going to starve to death or if he had a plan to do her in another way. He then took a seat on the large brown leather couch next to Ellen. "So now tell me my dear", he growled, "what have you learned so far about the Nazi's and what have you written about so far? You asked me what I want and this is it." Ellen tried to speak but she was so nervous that her dry mouth kept her from speaking loudly. "Speak up", he shouted. "I can't", cried Ellen, "my mouth is too dry". "Very well", he huffed and went to the kitchen cupboard and retrieved a glass. He went over to the bar and poured some water. She was glad he didn't put ice in it because she was still cold, and shaking from nerves, but ice would have been a sociable nicety and she didn't think he knew anything about that or just plain didn't care. "Now then, my dear, you were about to say"..., and Ellen said, "This book isn't about you". The next thing Ellen knew was that Van Eyck/Vermeer jumped from his seat and slapped her violently across her face. "Now, now, my dear", he said with hatred in his eyes, "You don't possibly expect me to believe that, do you?" "Yes, I do!" she yelled. She instantly regretted her flip remark because a second resounding slap arrived across her face. This time he had split her lip open and she could taste blood running down her mouth. "I think you should be more reasonable in your responses my dear. I am anything but stupid." She was totally repulsed by his "my dears", and knew that she had acted inappropriately to a madman. So she altered her strategy.

"Look", Ellen tried to explain calmly, "Yes, I got the initial idea because of you and your wife, but that is where the similarity ends". "I always wondered, quite honestly if you did have something to do with the Nazi's because of your immigration to Argentina and then to the United States, your denial about anything German – even though you speak predominantly German, and to be perfectly open, you and were wife's behavior has been anything but normal. But that was it".

Van Eyck/Vermeer eyed her madly and then said with a glint in his eye, "Yes, but you see my dear, now the spotlight has been placed on me. "But I didn't use your last name", cried Ellen. "You don't have to worry". "You described us to a tee and you didn't have to use our names for people to get wondering about us", Van Eyck/Vermeer explained angrily. "I think you are getting ahead of yourself", said Ellen. Again the slap was immediate and painful. This time her head rang like a bell and she didn't know how long she was going to be able to stay conscious if this kept up. Not only had she never been treated like this before but also her mind was racing to know how to answer without getting hit. So far, she wasn't doing too well. Her head hurt, her lip throbbed and she didn't know how long she could keep it together without going to pieces. Maybe, she opined, maybe that was his goal. Who knew with a crazy person? There wasn't a manual written to tell you what to do in this kidnapped condition.

Agent Malone was speeding up the Thruway and not keeping it at the speed limit. In the meantime, the Albany agent who had been doing their research had called Mrs. Penn back and once again reiterated that she was to stay in her house, not contact any one. The agent then said that she had given them permission to liaise at her house before they tried to confront Van Eyck/Vermeer. Jeff thought that this was a great idea and as soon as they met up with the locals at the Thruway stop, they would head toward the Penn's home. As Malone and Portman pulled into the Thruway stop they spotted three police cars. Nothing much happened this far north and the officers were pumped for some excitement. Jeff was resentful of their enthusiasm because of Ellen but understood that they didn't get to see much action so he had to go along with their mood. The officers spread out a map of Lake Bern on the hood of Malone's sedan and showed them where the Van Eyck/Vermeer home was located. And just south of his place was the Penn's. They too had a five acre plot with woods, lake frontage, and lots of privacy. The FBI agents explained that they would approach the house and use the other policemen for back-up. They had no idea if he was even there. But they were hoping he was and that this could end peacefully but after Jeff had seen the lengths that this madman had gone to, to date, he had his doubts. They wasted no time and all four cars headed to the Penn's home on Lake Bern. If it hadn't been such a serious situation, Jeff and Michael would have enjoyed the ride to the lake.

The Adirondack's were a beautiful scene. The woods and lakes and mountains were so picturesque. This was the Rockies on a smaller scale – but still quite beautiful. The officers arrived at the Penn home and found Mrs. Penn questioningly waiting at the front door with a quizzical look on her face. "All I've been told is there could be something going on at the Vermeer's and that I should stay in doors", she said. "I wanted to call my husband but the agent told me not to. So, what is going on"? Agents Malone and Portman took turns adding bits of information briefly and explained that Dr. Vermeer might just be involved in the disappearance of a capital district woman. Mrs. Penn seemed totally shocked but not totally surprised. "I always felt there was something weird about people who were so unfriendly" she said. Agent Malone asked Mrs. Penn if she could draw a crude map of the inside of the Vermeer's home. She squinched up her nose and thought for a moment. "We were over there several times when they were building it, and I know the basic layout, but I don't know if there have been any alterations to it. "That's good enough", said Jeff. So she grabbed a note pad and drew in from memory where the different rooms were. The guest bedrooms were on the first floor where the garages were. There was also a very large bathroom down there too. The driveway swept down the back of the property and there was a simple solid door that could enter into the garages. That was the only entry into the house that they could tell. They thought it odd when they were building it that it only had one true door. On the second floor with vaulted two story ceilings there was a very large open living room/great room with a to-die-for view. The kitchen was behind that room and also open. It was more like a very large galley kitchen with a large island/bar separating the appliances from the rest of the area. The master bedroom was also on this level as was the laundry room and large master bath. There was a massive wall of mudstone which served as the wall for the fireplaces. There was one fireplace in a common sitting area on the first floor and directly above it and between all of the glass sliders on the second floor there was a massive fireplace that looked quite Bavarian. It would not be a difficult house to reconnoiter but the agents didn't know if anything had been changed. In all it was at least 6500 square feet, a far cry from the modest bungalow in Rochester. They thanked Mrs. Penn for all of her in-put and then started to leave. "Oh, and another thing," she added. "The Vermeer's are the only family on the lake who do not have a fancy name plate or a catchy address post. We are 532 but we call our home Hidden Knoll, because we built on the highest point of our land and you can't really see much of the house from the road. The Vermeer's are just 534 on their mailbox. But it is just the very next house up the road. They thanked her again and told her they would report back to her to let her know what had happened. She watched them leave with that same quizzical look and then shut the door. She thought to herself, "My, my, wouldn't that be something! Here I've lived next to a "maybe" criminal all these years and didn't know it. I wonder who he really is or was."

Ellen's mind was racing to try to come up with a plan. She was tied to the chair, couldn't move, was hungry and thirsty, throbbed from her head and was desperately trying to think. She tried to think of way to respond to him and keep him talking, so maybe he would calm down. But she knew he was crazy or else she wouldn't be in this mess. "Look", she soothed, "I'm sure you are perfectly safe. The only people who could possibly know about the plot of this book and wonder about you are the relatives". Then she realized what she had just said. She almost lost it and screamed at him.

Van Eyck/Vermeer just scorned her. "So, you see what my predicament is. Now, some one has to pay for this situation. I loose my lake home which I just love, I have to relocate my operation, and I'll need a new identity." Tough shit, thought Ellen. But she was smart enough at that moment not to open her mouth. "Your operation?" queried Ellen. "Oh, yes", said Van Eyck/Vermeer, "now that you are not going to live to talk, I guess I can explain. You are like the Jews and the unwanted –expendable or should I say exterminable", he said and then cackled his hideous laugh. Pompously he paced in front of the vast sliders which faced the lake. He decided to pull the sheers now that it was getting dark. As he was kneeling at the fire place, he started making a fire. He also started to tell Ellen who he was and what he was all about. "You see, my dear, my name is not Willem Van Eyck or Pieter Vermeer. Those are just aliases as you people say. No, my name is really Edmond Schmitt and my wife was actually named Karla. My wife and I were children of the Third Reich. My uncle was one of the highest placed men in Hitler's tightly knit group. He was a dedicated and committed Nazi. My wife, who was four years older than I, and I were just out of medical school in 1942 and we both had become pediatricians. My uncle, who was very proud of me for being so bright and so intellectually advanced, having graduating from medical school at the age of 23, was working with one of his best friends, Heinrich Himmler. When Himmler set up his first concentration camp, in Dachau, in 1933, my uncle was right there beside him working to better the blood of The Deutschland. And he made sure that we got a plum assignment in Himmler's upper echelon of researchers." He smiled arrogantly.

"The purpose of the pure blood of the Aryan race was to cleanse the population and get as pure a Nordic or Aryan gene pool as possible. We wanted our blond haired blue eyed intelligent beauties. This meant the immediate extermination of all sub-humans. We are talking about the Slavs in Poland and Russia, the Gypsies, homosexuals, Jehovah's Witnesses, Jews, the disabled and sickly, the mentally ill, and alcoholics. Our job was to maintain the purist German Master Race possible. And it didn't matter if we had a little fun when we experimented. You see, most men and women were immediately destroyed – put down like dogs – after they were stripped of their possessions – even their gold teeth – they were taken into the ovens or shot and buried in mass graves. This was not loss for the world, it was only going to make it better." Ellen didn't care if she got hit, so she piped up and told him "You're crazy, you bastard". Once again she got it right across the face with a ferocious blow. Ellen put her head back on the chair and tried to get her vision back to normal.

"Before you rudely interrupted me, I was telling you about my illustrious medical career which was only interrupted by the fall of the Fuhrer". He ranted as if Ellen hadn't said a word. "Klara and I enjoyed our cutting edge research. You see, the Third Reich was already alive and active before WWII. It lasted in its glory days from 1933 to 1945. Ah, those were the days. We were in control of so many people and we were going to become not only the Master Race, but control the whole world", he raved on almost as if Ellen didn't exist and he was teaching students in class.

"Josef Mengele, one of our idols, was doing research on twins at Auschwitz. He developed interesting experiments by devising physical torments to see what the results were. After all they were Jewish twins, so it didn't matter. Klara and I decided to duplicate his work. Not only did we work on children but we worked on adults, too. When the Jews would get off the trains, we would select out the men from the women. The healthy ones were kept to either do work or be research subjects. The children were either destroyed or used also. "You would be surprised how long a person could live while being tortured," he laughed. "I knew they were all crazy", thought Ellen. They were cold and heartless with no conscience but with expert efficiency. They seemed to be true sociopaths, but unfortunately with great intelligence and cunning.

"All of our friends in Dachau had a great time. We were living very well because of our status and were convinced that we would win the war because of our superior intellect and our strength. But unfortunately we underestimated the Americans joining the Allies. When the war appeared to be coming to an end and not in our favor, all of us decided to get out of Germany and continue our work elsewhere. Many of us made it out of Germany and into Italy. There Klara and I arranged through a distant cousin to get a boat to Africa and then on to Argentina. We heard that that is where several of our comrades had gone. Argentina was a beautiful country and we enjoyed the weather. When we arrived in Argentina we were ecstatic that not only were we welcomed by the Argentineans, but we found such a large number of our friends who had been able to escape also. In fact we socialized with them and continued to enjoy German company." He continued explaining that they were able to socialize with their idol, Josef Mengele, in Argentina before he moved on to Brazil. They were saddened when they heard of his suspicious death from drowning in 1979. Before this, though, they learned that the Nazi movement needed them in the United States, and led Klara and I to make the decision to immigrate into America with a false identity. We were beginning to think that the Nazi hunters might be getting too hot on our trail. When we came to America we brought our daughter, who you know, and she became a total American. Her English is perfect and she acclimated perfectly. That is not surprising because she is German after all." Ellen thought for a moment and then asked, "Then how did you let her marry an Italian." "My daughter doesn't know about our past. We are no longer in Germany and we have to be discreet. Our daughter decided that she wanted to marry your brother in-law because he would make a good provider and she wouldn't have to worry about her future.

She wanted to stay in America and we had always secretly hoped to return to the Motherland and retire there. But that didn't work out. My daughter does not know that we were such highly regarded physicians and researchers."

"When we were newly arrived in Argentina, some of the higher Nazi leaders came to Klara and I and asked us to help with the future development of the Nazi party and movement. We worked behind the scenes there and then when we informed them of our move to the United States they asked us to continue our work here. I am not a janitor as every one believes. And Klara was not a simple seamstress. I work at the Millabro Company, but I am the head of the office not the cleaning man. My Millabro Company is the office of the further development of Nazism and of the betterment of the Aryan race. And I am in charge. You would be surprised the number of like minded people in this country. Nazism isn't dead. Oh, no, far from it. How do you think your "skinheads" get all of their information and support? But you have to understand, some work is never done," and he looked off dreamily.

As he finished his explanation, he turned to Ellen and said, "So you see my dear, I have gone to a great deal of time and expense to allow myself a safe passage to my new destination. My office is packing up lock, stock, and barrel, even as we speak. It's such a pity really. I loved this lake and its peacefulness; it reminded me of some of the spots I knew in Bavaria with all of the pine trees and water. But my new location has a similar setting out west and I shall have a new adventure building my new home. In fact I am going to try to replicate this one.

"And alas, you must now disappear for ever. I am going to wait until quite late and then I am going to put you peacefully in the nice big hole I had dug supposedly for a Jacuzzi. I cleverly allowed all of the leaves to fall in to it so that not only will you go unnoticed but after I put all the dirt over you, I will put the leaves back on top and no one will ever be the wiser. I will sell the house next spring and you will be comfortably resting forever at the base of the lake. Such a lovely resting spot! You are quite lucky! Most people just get a crowded plot in a wide open area, or an oven, but you, my dear, will be looking out upon this beautiful lake for every season" he sneered wickedly.

Ellen knew that he meant it. She silently cried and tried to rock as she sobbed. She felt so totally helpless. No one would know where she was and worse yet, no one would ever know what happened to her. Van Eyck just cackled at her and sat down to wait for the dead of night. Ellen wondered if there were any way that she could possibly get out of this chair but the tape was wrapped tightly around her arms just above the elbows. Her hands were slightly moveable but she had nothing available to even try to cut the tape. All she could do was wait and despair. She thought of her husband and her boys. She knew she was going to miss their college graduations, their weddings, the grandbabies. She wouldn't get to grow old with Daniel and hopefully enjoy retirement if Daniel could ever give up his work. She thought of all of the happy moments in her life. She remembered fondly her wedding, her family, the births of her sons, so many of their accomplishments and of how proud she was of them. She had stopped sobbing, but tears still continued to streak her face at each new memory. She was exhausted and surprised that she could make more tears because she was so dehydrated. Her mouth was dry but her face was wet. From her hypothermia-like experience in the trunk, to the sheer terror and grief that she was now feeling, she thought she just might die of a broken heart right there, right now. And all of this was happening to her, she thought, because she was a bored housewife and decided to write books. She rued the day that she ever made that decision. She knew that her second book was just about ready to send to the publisher, and the money – if any – from it would help defray the costs of her sons' education and future as the first one did. All she could do now was wait for the end.

CHAPTER 11

THE AGENTS AND officers asked permission to leave their vehicles in the large circular drive at the Penn's. She had told them that that was fine and so they all left on foot with a basic plan in mind. They were just going to try to get a good look at the house before they barged in. They didn't know if he was in residence or if Ellen was with him so they decided to be prudently quiet and check out the area. As they approached the large home, they smelled smoke. But, they didn't know if it was coming from Van Eyck/Vermeer's or was a co-mingling of smells from the other homes on the road. As soon as the house came into sight, they saw smoke flowing from the fireplace chimney. This was a good sign. He at least may be there.

Jeff had arranged for the officers to remain behind the trees at the south side of the drive and wait for their report. Jeff planned to try the one and only door into the house and Malone was going to try to see in the sliders which opened onto a deck which spread all the way across the front of the house that looked out at the lake. With cat-like creeping, both Jeff and Malone went about their tasks. First Jeff tried the door, which was definitely locked and then he proceeded around the North side of the house. Malone took the South side and was soon on the deck.

There were opaque sheers pulled across the sliders, but it still allowed for some view into the living room. At first he saw a large man pacing around the fireplace and then he saw a woman tied to a chair. Ellen. Quietly he crept down the stairs and back to the waiting Jeff and officers. Mrs. Penn had been right. All curtains were drawn on the house except for the sliders. Malone told them that there were sheers drawn over the sliders but that he did indeed see Van Eyck/ Vermeer in the living room. Jeff already knew that, because Malone had given him the thumbs up sign as he was approaching the group which told him that they were a go. After a few moments of concurring, four officers went with Malone to try to get in the sliders by surprise and two of the officers were going to go with Jeff as backup through the door into the garage. Jeff was going to wait for the noise of breaking glass before he broke the door in to the garage.

In order not to make noise, Malone showed the officers how to shinny up the hand rail on the stairs. Stairs notoriously squeak and he didn't want to let anyone know that they were there. So he once again shinnied up the railing which was no easy task. Fortunately they all had their gloves on and it helped with the splinters. As Malone was peeking around the edge of the first slider, he noticed that Van Eyck/Vermeer was seated now and it looked as if he was trying to rest his eyes. Ellen was still taped to the chair and looked miserably sad and afraid. Malone signaled for the other men to come up to him. The plan was that Malone was going to shoot out the sliding glass door and crash in as soon as the glass was shattered.

Sliding glass doors have two layers of glass which are adhered to the rim of the metal or wood. Breaking them is not easy.

Malone's plan of entry into the living room was to shoot two consecutive shots into the windows but away from Ellen. He was planning on angling his shots so that he wouldn't strike anybody. He saw that Van Eyck/Vermeer was dozing and so he could use the element of surprise. As soon as the four officers were directly behind him with their guns drawn, he took his aim. He fired two very quick shots into the glass and immediately had his right arm up to protect his face and burst through the glass door. As he leapt he heard the sound of shattering glass particles and the spider web of hundreds of fissures gave way to his weight. As he bounded into the living room, he was preparing to pounce on Van Eyck/Vermeer. However, he was not totally asleep and jumped with the precision of a cat. In an instant, instead of being able to wrestle him to the ground, Malone saw that Van Eyck/Vermeer had his hand at Ellen's throat and gleaming in the light was a knife. He said, "Don't come any closer or I'll slit her throat like a slaughtered pig." Malone froze. Agent Malone waved for his officers to stand down. He then tried to talk to Van Eyck/Vermeer. He started by saying, "Let's not do anything hasty". Van eyck/Vermeer merely sneered at Malone and said, "Yes, let's not do anything hasty. I have plans to leave here and now I am taking Ellen with me as an insurance policy." He switched hands with the knife but kept his forearm around Ellen's throat in a death grip and Malone could see Ellen gasping for breath. All of the officers and Malone had dropped their guns to their sides but did not holster them. Quickly Van Eyck/Vermeer slashed the tape with a surgically sharp knife which was keeping Ellen in the chair. He stroked twice with his knife and she was then free and pulled from the chair with remnants of the tape across the front of her. Now he had her right in front of him. He started to back away from Malone and the officers when he heard a voice from behind him. It was Jeff. "Stop where you are and release the lady", Jeff warned angrily. "Well, well, well. I guess we have a Mexican standoff here, gentlemen. But I warn you, the first move toward me and she dies. All I want is to leave here peacefully." Jeff remained immobile and using his hostage crisis skill taught at the academy, he tried again to reason with him. "You see, Mr. Van Eyck or Dr. Vermeer or whoever you are, you have no choice. You are totally outnumbered and you will die if you do not let Ellen go." "Ellen is it? You are on a first name basis, I see. What does her husband think of that?" he derided. "Your concern right now should be with your own life and not someone else's. You won't get two feet. Now lay down your knife and let Mrs. Dinato go." "No, you back off. I am an old man and not afraid to die. This woman has many years left but she means absolutely nothing to me. So you see, I have nothing to lose, now back off."

At this time Van Eyck/Vermeer's eyes were playing a game of ping pong. He would furtively glance at Malone and then back a Jeff, trying to see who was moving. Slowly Malone started to lift his gun. "Aah, aah, aah", Van Eyck/

Vermeer warned. Jeff was waiting for his opening. He was waiting for the second that Van Eyck/Vermeer looked over at Malone. The moment came. With lightening speed Jeff raised his gun and shot him in the head. The sudden impact caused Van Eyck/Vermeer to gasp but then lose the ability to hold the knife or Ellen. The look on his face was one of surprise but Jeff knew that Van Eyck/Vermeer knew that this had to be the outcome. He may have hoped for outsmarting them but that was such a long shot. He knew he was dead before the bullet left the barrel. He slumped to the floor but his weight took Ellen down too. For an instant Jeff thought that he had made a terrible mistake and that he had also somehow shot Ellen, too. Then he heard her crying and trying to squirm out from under him. She was so shaky that she drunkenly stumbled. Jeff rushed to help her and was able to get her upright and in his arms. He hugged her tightly and was almost weak kneed himself. He was so relieved that she was safe.

He just stood there holding her and trying to calm her. She sobbed and was hysterical. He soothed her and rocked her back and forth like a newborn. "It's all over now, you are going to be fine." The smell of cordite hung in the area and the room suddenly seemed claustrophobic. Jeff motioned to Malone and the others to leave for a little while and let Ellen calm down. Malone asked the officers to accompany him outside and prepare to notify their respective offices and to call for the coroner and the lab. It was obvious that Van Eyck/Vermeer was dead and wasn't going anywhere and he also was aware that Jeff and Ellen needed some privacy. Malone also wanted to call Daniel and tell him the good news.

After the others left, Jeff led Ellen over to the couch away from the body. He purposely placed her with her back to the mess of what was left of Van Eyck/Vermeer. They sat still until Ellen could compose herself. Finally she stopped sobbing and was left with just the hiccuppy-like breaths that are a result of crying so hard. Continually Jeff stroked her hair and calmed her down, soothing her gently. She was so relieved to be safe and to be comforted so tenderly. She hadn't felt this cared for and adored in a long time. Jeff had his handkerchief out cleaning off her face and helping her blow her nose. She asked, "Do you do this for all of your hostages?" He just smiled gently at her and held her close. "Ellen, you are so dear to me. You are the kind of woman I have been looking for all of my life. You are kind and considerate. You make a lovely home and you would make me fat with your cooking. But most of all you are the most nurturing person I have ever met. You care so deeply for others. Your selflessness is amazing. Even though she was a nervous wreck, she still blushed. "I love you Ellen."

At that moment, all Ellen wanted to do was to feel his lips on hers and just bury herself in his arms. She felt so safe, so protected and so cherished. "This is all a woman ever wants, she thought". At this moment she had to make one of the biggest decisions in her life. She was so tempted. She ached to be held by him, to make love to him. She wanted to drown in his kisses. But she sadly realized that Jeff could never be hers, Jeff told her that everything was going to be OK. "No, Jeff, it won't be OK. Nothing will ever be OK. I love you too and I can't have you. Jeff said, "You can have me but it is you I can't have. See, that is why I love you so much. You're honorable and true. Why am I not surprised?" She calmed again and she looked up into his eyes. She saw love that she hadn't seen in such a long time. She saw longing and restraint. She truly loved him.

They sat there quietly enmeshed in each other hoping that time could stand still. But Malone had returned and was announcing that he was ready to take them back to the Dinato's. Malone drove and Jeff sat in the back seat with Ellen. She laid her head in his lap and was asleep before they got to the thruway. Before she knew it, they were slowing and going over gravel and she knew they were home.

Malone went in to warn Daniel and Frankie that Ellen looked very bruised and assaulted but that she would be OK. He also was giving Jeff and Ellen one last moment to say good-bye. Jeff helped Ellen out of the car and they stood there under the harsh scrutiny of the emergency alarm light. He held her hands in his and looked at her, as if he would never be the same again. Ellen looked back in the same way. Both of their hearts were breaking. But both knew what the right thing to do was. Ellen reached up and placed a tender kiss on his cheek. She lingered close to his face and felt his warm breath on her skin. "How can I ever thank you?" whispered Ellen. "You have given me my life back, my family back. And you" Jeff just smiled a half smile. They stood there not knowing what to do or say next. But the silence was broken by the garage door rushing open. They immediately parted hands and stood there watching the joy and relief on Daniel and Frankie's faces. Both of them grabbed Ellen up and hugged her. Frankie couldn't help himself and he silently cried. Daniel had tears in his eyes and let Frankie vent his emotions. "God, Mom, I'm glad you're OK. When I came home and saw that you weren't here, I didn't think I would ever see you again." Frankie hugged her tight again. Daniel said, "And I was scared out of my wits. There are so many things I haven't told you recently. And I have been so tied up with work. But things are going to change, you'll see. When I thought I lost you forever, I was beside myself. Just ask Frankie." "Yeah, Mom, I've seldom seen dad cry and he really lost it."

Malone spoke up and told the Dinato's that they were going to leave. They had a mountain of paper work to do and they knew that Ellen needed some first aid, to eat and then get some well deserved rest. As Daniel was shaking their hands and thanking them for saving his wife, he noticed the way Jeff and Ellen were looking at each other. He saw the longing. He saw the bittersweet good-bye in their eyes. "Yes, there are going to be some changes around here. In fact you may just get tired of me being around the house so much." Ellen smiled and bid the agents good-bye and again a thank you. The family with their arms around Ellen walked back into the garage and the agents got into their car.

Malone glanced over at Jeff when they were back on the highway again. He had a faraway look in his eyes and was lost in thought. "I'm sorry, man. I know you were really taken with her," Malone appeased. "If she were free

I would just jump at the chance. She is exactly the kind of woman I have always wanted to marry. She is "the one". But she is not free and there is nothing that I can do about it." Malone was quiet for a while. He really didn't know how to console him so he decided that he would just give him time. Finally he broke his silence and told Jeff, "It is like a death in a way. When you love someone, even briefly, it is a death when you can't be with them and have them haunting your memories. You can grieve and it will take time, but you will come out of the haze. And besides, I'm here for you buddy." "Thanks," said Jeff but he kept silent. The ride back to the office was uncomfortable and awkward. But they parted ways and told each other that they would see each other tomorrow.

Jeff got into his own car and drove home slowly to his dark, lonely apartment. He let himself in and dropped his keys on the entry table and shucked his coat and holster. He sat in the dark for a long time, not wanting to move and feeling miserable.

After the family had a meal that had been brought over by the neighbors and Frankie talked Ellen's ear off, Daniel saw that her eyes were glassing over from fatigue. Frankie excused himself and went to bed. There were phone calls to the boys away at school and she reassured them that she was just fine but looked a little weird. The boys were relieved and happy and knew very little about her ordeal. She promised to fill them in tomorrow and on their next visit up to Vermont to college. Now it was Daniel who was trying to talk to her, but Ellen just held up her hand and said, "Now that I have a full stomach,

I need to go to bed. We can talk tomorrow". "Of course, what was I thinking?" He ushered her upstairs by holding on to her arm. She tried to wash her face but had to be careful because of the bruises and abrasions. She then put on ointment but it couldn't help the black eye that was sprouting around her eye. She finally crawled into bed. Daniel was not asleep which was atypical. Usually the instant his head hit the pillow, he was out like a light. No pillow talk, no sentimentality. No touching – just roommates. But tonight Daniel propped himself on his elbow and watched her trying to sleep. He stroked her hair and she was surprised. She silently wondered about his behavior. Maybe this shock was just what he needed to make him appreciate her, but was it too late? She closed her eyes and went off to sleep. Daniel watched her for several minutes and finally fell asleep having thought about how he could win back her affection. She knew how Ellen felt about Jeff. After all he had gone into a dangerous situation and saved her. He was her knight in shining armor. How could he compete with that? Daniel began to make plans in his head about what he could do to show her that she was his special wife. He would start dating her again and he would prove to her that she had made the right choice with him. This was going to be his new focus and he knew that he had his job cut out for him. He even dreamed about things he could do for Ellen.

The next day Frankie was forced to go to school but he was looking forward to telling all his friends about his mom's harrowing ordeal. Daniel didn't go to work and stayed home to help Ellen. She awoke sore and achy. Her face looked like it had been used for batting practice. Daniel waited on her and tried to be helpful. But he found she was withdrawn and quiet. He tried to talk to her but she told him that she just wanted to be quiet. Most of the morning, they just sat by the fire and read. At lunch, Daniel tried to fix a fancy lunch but it looked more like something that a five year old would fix. But she giggled and told him that it was very sweet and very unusual. She really meant it. It was quite unusual for Daniel to help out, let alone fix her a meal. She had never been treated like a queen. She had always been on call even when she had the flu. She rarely took to her bed. So she never knew what it was like to be waited on. She did all the caring. That afternoon, Ellen took a nap and Daniel busied himself in his office at home. When Frankie came home from school, he and Daniel spent some time talking in his office. Ellen emerged from upstairs and found the two deep in conversation. "Can I join, asked Ellen?" They both looked up in surprise. "Of course, come on in." they said. "God, Mom. You look awful said Frankie. "Thanks", Ellen said sarcastically. "Well, I mean, you really look like you've been beaten up." "I have", chuckled Ellen. "Yea, that is a bit obvious", he said apologetically. So what should we do about dinner?" she asked. "While you were asleep I ordered a dinner catered. It should be here in about an hour"

Ellen marveled at the change. Daniel had never done anything like this. He was a stickler for home cooking. He didn't like to go out to eat because he did so much of it in business. This was a true treat. "Why don't we have a glass of wine and some cheese and crackers while we wait," suggested Daniel. They all agreed. Since Daniel was Italian, he had served the boys wine ever since they could walk. They usually had sips, but as they aged they were allowed to have wine with dinner. By the time they went away to school, there was no mystique in drinking and they didn't go off the deep end like so many of their classmates. They knew how to drink and drink responsibly. Frankie was no exception. Frankie enjoyed his wine and asked Ellen more questions. His classmates had questions he couldn't answer so he wanted to be able to tell them the answers.

The doorbell rang and Daniel went to see if it was the caterer. He returned with his arms full of warmed food and the caterer followed him into the kitchen with balloons and flowers. The balloons said "Congratulations". He explained that he couldn't get a balloon that said "Yeah, you made it", or, "You survived!", so these would have to do. For the first time Ellen laughed her usual hearty laugh. Daniel was grateful for that.

They dined in the dining room and Daniel even lit candles. Ellen was telling the guys that she could get used to this. She thought aloud, "Maybe I should be kidnapped more often. Frankie and Daniel both loudly protested and laughed, which made her feel wanted and loved. They were just finishing dinner when the phone rang. Daniel answered and it was Jeff. Daniel listened to what was obviously an invitation to come down to the office. Daniel said he would have to decline because he was going back to work. He explained that Ellen had insisted on him going back and that she didn't need to be babysat.

She wanted things to get back to normal. He handed the phone to Ellen and she heard Jeff's voice. "How are you feeling", he asked. "Like I have been hit by a truck", said Ellen. "Do you feel up to coming down to the office and making a formal statement? I thought that you would appreciate a day of rest before we threw you into the ugly details," he said.

"Sure", she said, "I would appreciate getting out of the house. I have to get back to living". "Well, we'll see you at ten tomorrow morning". "Thank you", she said. His tone was just business, nothing personal. She was so bewildered that she didn't know what to do. Ellen excused herself after thanking the guys for such a nice treat and told them she was going to get ready for bed and take another hot bath for her aches and then she was going to read for a while. They both told her that she deserved it and they would be up a little later. As Ellen lazed in the bubbles of her tub, she thought about Jeff and Daniel. She mulled over the attributes of both men. She finally decided that meeting Jeff was a gift. She wouldn't have missed the thrill, the excitement, the heart quickening of meeting someone who adored her. But she knew that he was just a reminder of what she all ready had. It actually came down to passion or the past. She ruminated that that must be what happens to people who have a mid-life crisis. The idea of gaining instant romance and pitching a long history of caring and sharing is too enticing for most. She almost had become a statistic for the eager and the restless. Fortunately, she realized and let a level head lead instead of her hungry heart. Daniel had shared the birth and the raising of three wonderful boys. He may have drifted off because of his work, but she was taking stock of what she could do to put the romance back in their marriage. It was a two way street.

Ellen realized that the reality was that she hadn't invested in her marriage either. She had allowed Daniel to drift. She was determined to make her marriage stronger and better and put herself out there for Daniel. It did take two to tango. But she also knew anew what it felt like to have a longing heart and she knew that it would take her awhile to get Jeff Portman out of her thoughts. She also understood that she had made the right decision; morally, spiritually, and sensibly. She chuckled at herself for being so pragmatic but after all, she could still look at herself proudly in the mirror. She was going to grow old with the man she had made a promise to at the altar, oh, so many years ago. This she mused was what those vows were all about. 'Til death do us part – no matter what. Biblically and historically she now knew what it must have been like when crops failed, misfortune attacked, and temptation abounded. Love – no matter what phase it was in, still had the hold on most people.

The next morning, life seemed to be back to a more normal routine. They ate breakfast together and Frankie went off to school. Daniel stopped in the doorway that led to the garage and wished Ellen a good day – as usual, but this time he walked back over to her and hugged her carefully and kissed her sincerely. "Mmmmm", purred Ellen. I wish you didn't have to go". "Either do I, but there is this weekend and we are going to visit the boys up at school and you know that Frankie always stays with one of the boys, so the hotel room will be all ours". He winked and he was off.

Ellen really didn't want to go to the FBI office. She didn't want to see Jeff. She didn't want to be reminded of what could have been if she had stepped over that line. As she drove she tried not to think of him. But her mind kept drifting back to him. "The forbidden fruit", she mused. She was Eve in the garden and she was tempted. But she also knew that she had a husband and three sons who would depend on her to do the right thing. "Maybe in another life," she sighed. She knew that she was not the kind of woman to have an affair. And getting a divorce and rending her vows and her commitment to her family was so painful that she knew she could not go there. Her trip into to this office was filled with ping pong thoughts but she kept running the mantra that she had made the right choice.

When she arrived at the office and walked into the reception area, Jeff was standing there waiting for her. She was surprised and thought that maybe he would be at his desk. "Ellen, I'm glad you could come. Before we go into my office I thought I would tell you a few things about this case". '"All business", she thought, "just as well." "To begin with, I never really told you the reason for our first visit. (Our visit – keep it business like.) You see, there is a covert agent who has been doing work for us for a long time. He is quite good, but unfortunately for him, you kind of blew his cover. He has had to come in out of the cold, as they say, and he is retiring. He, as the character in your book, also had drops and covert activities and was never uncovered. But when your book came out, it was way too close to his modus operandi. So he is finished as an agent for us. In fact, his code name is really and ironically, "The Crow". She looked at Jeff unbelieving. This couldn't be!!!!! Would you like to meet him?" "Sure, said Ellen. "But will he be mad at me?" she asked sheepishly.

"No, I think he was getting burned out from all of the secrecy and stealthy activity. It takes a toll you know. No, he was thinking of getting out for the last few years and this was the impetus that it took to make him come to his decision. So it is just the opposite, he is relieved to be able to retire and return to a more normal life style."

Jeff led Ellen into his office. Jeff's chair was swiveled so that it faced the window. All she could see was the top of the Crow's head. Jeff cleared his throat as an interruption and proceeded. "Excuse me. I would like to introduce you to the author who wrote the book about you. Slowly the chair swiveled around so that she could see him.

There sat her husband, Daniel. "What???, she screeched. Is this some kind of sick joke?" Daniel slowly rose from the chair and he walked over to her. "No, this isn't a dirty trick. I am the Crow and I am now officially retired". "But how, why, I can't believe you have hidden this from me all of these years. How could I have dreamed this whole thing????"

"There are a lot of explanations and a lot of questions to answer", he said. "But now I am taking you to a lovely lunch and we are going to spend the afternoon planning a cruise. I will still work in business but this monkey business is finished. I am going to be concentrating on the woman I love". Ellen was so shocked she didn't know what to say. The two just stood there and hugged, gigglng like two newlyweds.

Jeff stood there admiring this couple. It was so nice to see a couple bonded forever. It would take him a while to heal his heart, but he knew this was the right thing. He thought to himself, "I am going to concentrate on my life and my future retirement and looking for "the one". Hopefully she is still out there".

CPSIA information can be obtained
at www.ICGtesting.com
Printed in the USA
LVHW042203140920
666021LV00002B/612